Fetish
Fantastic

D1615790

Fetish Fantastic

tales of power and lust
from futuristic to surreal

Edited By
Cecilia Tan

Circlet Press, Inc.
Cambridge, MA

Fetish Fantastic
edited by Cecilia Tan

Copyright © 1999 by Circlet Press, Inc.
Cover art & Design Copyright © 1997 by Michael Manning
All Rights Reserved

Printed in Canada

First Edition March 1999

ISBN 1-885865-13-9

Individual copyrights to the works represented in this volume are held
by the respective authors and artists of the works.

This text cannot be distributed, reproduced, transcribed, photocopied,
uploaded, downloaded, or otherwise transmitted or transformed into
similar or any other media without the explicit written consent of the
Authors and Publisher. (Excerpts of up to 200 words may be used for
purposes of review.)

Circlet Press is distributed in the USA and Canada by the LPC Group.
Circlet Press is distributed in the UK and Europe by Turnaround Ltd.
Circlet Press is distributed in Australia by Bulldog Books.

For a catalog, information about our other imprints, review copies, and
other informtaion, please write to:

Circlet Press, Inc.
1770 Massachusetts Avenue, #278
Cambridge, MA 02140
circlet-info@circlet.com
http://www.circlet.com

Table of Contents

Introduction

If you're reading this book for the sex (and I hope that you are...) and don't enjoy the form of foreplay known as delayed gratification, then skip this introduction now, and read it at the end while you're lying in your proverbial sweaty sheets (or among your cast-off chains, tangled whips, or what have you).

Still reading?

When it comes to "fantastic" fetishes, this book reflects a bias toward S/M, and the fetishes that associate around it: spanking, corsetry, corporal punishment, bondage, and other erotic turn-ons of the power exchange variety. You won't find much in here on foot fetishism (though maybe a bit on boots), and nothing on infantilism, Amazon giantesses, or other so-called "vanilla" fetishes. I leave the task of compiling that anthology to someone else—I've stuck with what I know. What I know is leather, boots, whips, dungeons, shackles, masters, slaves, dominas, and servants.

More than that, though, what I know are fantasies. Generally speaking, S/M is not about the objects or roles we fetishize, but the fantasies that imbue them with power. The whip is meaningless without the hand that swings it and, perhaps more importantly, the reason it is being swung. Were you a bad slave who needs to be punished? Are you a high-born heroine captured by pirates? Are you a religious acolyte seeking penitence? Or maybe something no one else has ever quite imagined?

These stories are in the "no one else has quite imagined" category. S/M as a means to climb the social ladder, S/M which liberates the mind, cyber-S/M, S/M as magic ritual, college degrees in S/M, S/M as art. But even as these stories push the envelope of futurism and fantasy, they have their basis in our current reality.

It is not a fantasy to imagine that S/M can be a positive and healthy force in the sexuality of a modern person. I have written many a political essay on why S/M is not violence and why fantasies of non-consensuality are liberating, and do not intend to paraphrase them here. But I should point out that one component of the much-trumpted leather community credo "safe, sane, consensual" is the knowledge of what is fantasy and what is not. When we play at S/M in the real world, our true fetish is for the scene itself, for the scenario of imaginary power we create between consenting partners. As such, the power which drives these stories is that intrinsic knowledge. Some stories will take the fantasy of imaginary nonconsent and run with it, while others will play with the border between consent and powerlessness. And no, I won't tell you which are which... that's for you to find out for yourself.

Have I teased you enough? I think so.

Cecilia Tan
Cambridge, MA

All Things Ripen
In Their Own Time
Reina Delacroix

Today is Friday, so I braid my chestnut hair back severely and tell the maid I am going out shopping. She nods, her mind already more on her coming hours of freedom inside the apartment than on any suppressed excitement she may sense in my voice. But I do not begrudge her the time I know she spends watching the simuus and drinking sake while I'm gone; I understand her need for escape a little too well.

I have a ritual for this day that focuses the anticipation at each critical moment. And my husband interrupted it first this morning, by announcing loudly at breakfast, "Tammi, yesterday Mr. Inoue came by my desk and asked me if we would complete a party he is having at his house."

I was silent for a moment, considering the implications of Charles's statement. I have never met Mr. Inoue, but I am well aware that he is second-in-line at my husband's company. The last-minute nature of the invitation means that a higher-status couple bowed out unexpectedly on him and we are being asked to fill out a particular number... no doubt one that the astronumerologists picked as auspicious for this date.

The numeris, as we call them, work now with computers rather than coins, and their copies of the astrological tables and I Ching are cross-indexed and hypertext-linked, but such is our renewed faith now in these otherwise unpredictable times that no one of stature makes a move without consulting them. If it is sometimes silently suspected that they may try to manipulate events into coming true, it is not unexpected that they will do so.

Sometimes, that is even desirable.

Anyway, the bad timing of this is another indication that after two years of hard work, we are still of relatively low status in my husband's company. And, as 'Rikis in a predominantly Nihi company, we accept this.

And yet, if we can accept this invitation, we will be seen as reliable and useful and eager—and can possibly displace this other unknown couple in the future.

This is a very difficult world we live in, inside the maze of companies that really control the New Sun Empire, and such an advantage cannot be passed up.

"Of course, Charles. When should I be ready?"

"Even allowing for being a few minutes late, you'd have to leave here no later than half past six. Mr. Inoue recognized the inconvenience of this sudden invite and suggested that I come straight home with him from the office, and he would have a car sent to pick you up."

That means I will have to cut my day short in order to get home in time. But both of these are great favors to us, since nonpublic transportation is rare in Lesser Kyoto. My sense that this invitation could be a springboard intensified.

"Also," Charles continued, "it seems that we and Mr. Inoue have the same numeri. Good fortune, that! It means you can easily find out what might be most suitable to wear to the party, so you don't clash with all the other guests."

Ah, everything is arranged, then. Now I must

arrange my own schedule to suit.

I decide I will not give up all of my day—it is my one moment of selfishness—but I do call the hairdresser to ask her to come early, and after that I follow as much of my normal ritual as possible.

I dress simply, in a navy blue silk shirt and trousers, and sandals. No jewelry; I am going shopping, after all, not meeting someone. The buttons seem big and clumsy, and I quickly remind myself there is nothing to be nervous about. I have done this a hundred times or more, and nothing has ever gone wrong.

Outside, I consider the weather and decide to walk everywhere on my own rather than use the treadways. There is still a low, cold mist lying around all the buildings, but it is intended purely to saturate the numerous plant boxes that dot the pavement. The overhead lamps will easily burn that off by midday.

Everything is carefully controlled in Lesser Kyoto; we may be living under a pressure dome on Earth's moon, but every inch of space the Nihis have laid out in their section has been considered both in a useful and an aesthetic sense. We are crowded—after all those years cramped together on their island, I doubt the Nihis would know any other way to live—but they have tried to make it as comfortable as possible within the limitations.

I drop by the grocer to order food for the next week and notice some beautiful tomatoes invitingly arranged on display. When I compliment him on their attractiveness, he smiles. "From Thaitown hydroponics. Expensive, but Thaitown is worth it."

"Good things always are," I reply politely.

He lifts one and hands it to me, along with a knife to cut it. "Try it. Please. I'm sure you will like it."

My hand trembles as I hold the knife and slide the blade into the red flesh to quarter it. It feels obscene to be doing this in public, and I take great pleasure in hiding how the action makes me feel. The fruit is fresh and juicy, and my mouth is so used to tart tomatoes from New Rome that it is an actual shock to taste sweetness and balance of texture where I have come to expect only faint bitterness and mushy meat.

"Oh, it's just wonderful. We will be celebrating tomorrow night"—i.e., if all goes well tonight, we will have friends over and joyously discuss every detail, every nuance of what was said at tonight's party—"and these would be perfect for it."

I move along my route now, the anticipation building with each step, added to now by the memory of enjoying the tomato. I go by the laundry to ask that our clothes be picked up, and the library to order new reading and sound for the next week... oh, certainly all these could be done through the computers, and in the 'Riki section probably would be. But the Nihis place great value on performing the formalities, and I find I enjoy these little rituals within the greater ritual of Friday.

This is my day out, and while it is as carefully arranged as the rest of my life (even the hours I will regretfully have to cut short today) at least it is arranged for me and no one else.

The pillared temple of the numeri Kumiko stands alone at the end of a cul-de-sac, stark white amidst the dark greens and greys and blacks of Lesser Kyoto's normal architecture. The bare white plastiwood common in these structures glows faintly even in the high lights of noon, due to the strongly phosphorescent dye used in coloring it... thus in the dark, a numeri's temple often has a haunted look. The white color is supposed to attract good spirits; more to the point, it makes them distinctive and easy to find for those in need of advice, at a price.

I enter the temple, leaving my sandals outside the angled archway, and the soft chimes on the door—no synthetic chimes here, or even one of glass that can be cheaply produced here at the factories, but a delicate metal mobile—announce my presence. I stop and wait politely on the mat, between the left and right openings into the hallways and in front of the large screen that closes off the far opening. "Gomen kudasai?"

Kumiko's soft voice calls from the back. "Tamara-san?"

"Yes, Kumiko-san."

"You are a few minutes early." Not tinged with reproach, just a statement of fact—and an oblique warning that she is not quite ready for me to come in further.

Depending on how important or connected the person consulting the numeri is, and also how well regarded the numeri's predictive talents are, even knowing precisely when someone visits a numeri could be quite a useful piece of knowledge to have about them or their business, and so numeris are very careful not to let clients run into each other at the temple.

When Charles was sponsored into the Amaterasu company by the retired Mr. Tanaka, he was kind enough also to give us a reference to Kumiko, who is regarded as one of the more skilled numeri. We are very lucky to have her guidance.

"I wished to spend a few moments meditating in your garden, Kumiko-san." Not a total lie, either: when I visit, I often step into her rock garden to think about what will happen next.

"I would be honored," she replies, and the curtains rustle as she returns to the back and her unknown client.

The garden is tiny, no more than 10' by 10', but the rocks build relentlessly from the low point as you enter to the high point across and the usual miniature waterfall is well placed just off center to the right. I sit half-lotus on the floor and close my eyes.

The image of the tomato in my hand, and how it felt

to hold the knife that opened it returns to me at once, and I realize how frightened I am of what I am about to do. Not just the normal fear of anticipation, either, but the nagging worry that I've never had to vary this part of my Friday ritual before—what if it can't be done?

What if this destroys the delicate balance, and this part—for this is the part I really wait for, the part I live for—cannot be done? Now, or ever again?

I notice a small grey-haired woman in a plain white kimono peering over the rocks at me. "Tamara-san? I had called you twice to say you are free to come in now, but you did not answer."

"Oh, I'm very sorry, Kumiko-san," I apologize as I follow her to her sitting room. "I guess I'm very worried about today."

She nods. "Yes, I already know that you have a very important invitation at the last minute. It was in the stars and the stones that this would happen."

"More like in your computer banks!" I think in a moment of irreverence, but I hold my tongue. Again I wonder how much of a numeri's success was due to pure foretelling and how much due to old-fashioned arranging of events to their liking.

And yet, even that second method would take a certain amount of predictive skills, that the arranged events would come out with the desired result, not just immediately, but in the long run. So in the end, did it matter whether Kumiko was a true magician or just an illusionist?

"Then you would also know that I have very little time to prepare for anything right now." I say quietly.

She nods again, and stares at me with her black eyes. "Yes, I already know you have only one hour to spend here. No more time for old Kumiko!" She laughs and smiles then, but her eyes are still intently fixed on mine. "Well, you have put yourself in my hands before and I have not failed you, have I?"

Failed me? No, Kumiko, you make everything possible. Everything.

She continues, "Yes, things will be have to be different this time, you know. What can be done in three hours cannot be done in one." And I realize she is referring to what is about to happen to me this afternoon, as well as what needs to be done for the evening.

"I know I can trust your arrangements, Kumiko-san," I say cautiously.

She smiles again, and without another word passing between us I arise and walk past her, to the back of the room where another screen hides an airlock built into the back of the house. Behind me I can hear her begin to tap away on the tiny keyboard that she keeps hidden in her lap, in the folds of her kimono.

Within the hour, she will have the proper dress for the party delivered to my house, along with the appropriate flowers and gift for the host, instructions to the hairdresser what style would look best... little details, all part of the greater ritual.

In the meantime...

I press my hand to the airlock's security system. The doors give way and I move into the middle chamber. The disinfectant cycle will only work coming from the other direction, so that no foreign matter contaminates Lesser Kyoto, but I do need to change.

I look at the clothes laid out for me to change into. Usually, I will wear an elaborate costume for this which fits in and makes me unrecognizable, but today it is only a thin white cotton blouse and short black skirt. In those, I will feel naked.

There is also a small jar of gold body paint on top of the clothes, and I slowly gild both my nipples and then, after a moment's hesitation, outline my labia with the paint as well. Then I dress and, taking a deep breath, go to the other door and wait for it to open.

On the other side of the wall from Kumiko's temple is the back side of the spaceport at Newton. The lock pops me out into a tiny closet on the other side, and I quickly go out into the main hallway so that I can mingle with the crowd getting off from the cattle-car shuttle.

The front part of the spaceport is reserved for dignitaries and rich businessmen; this is where the rest of the otherworldly travelers get off. And I, I too am a visitor from another world, though a much closer one than anyone watching would suspect.

He is waiting for me at the end of the hallway, standing dead still in the center of the hall as people walk around his powerful figure. This is already different; usually I just go directly to his room and do not see him before I close the door and shut the other world away.

He watches me walk down the hallway towards him, arms folded, no smile on his dark face, no sign of recognition except that his eyes are fixed on my movement. People are shouting and arguing and greeting wildly around us, and I just keep walking calmly towards him as if no one else were around, as if nothing else mattered.

It's not that I don't think of him during the rest of the week, wonder what his life is like outside of the hours he spends using me, but nothing prepares me for his physical existence except seeing him.

His name is Knife. That's all I know. All I need to know.

I stop a little more than an arm's length away from him. His eyes are cold as he looks me up and down. I am scared to death of him, and he knows it. He knows everything about me he needs to know.

Knife gets his name from the long scar on his left cheekbone, as well as from the black-handled weapons he wears on his sides, one in each scabbard. That scar streaks out livid under the harsh fluorescent lights. Even his brown skin looks more ashen than colored. But the eyes still are the same: wary but piercing.

"Kneel," he says in that firm, oddly dismissive way of his, leaving no room for argument on my part. It's as if he knows all the rules, but he also knows they just don't apply to him.

And maybe they don't.

I want to protest, but I can't, no sound comes from my mouth. Instead I kneel, and I begin to bow my head in shame, but his left hand grabs the braid at the back of my head and pulls on it so that I have to look up at his face and meet his gaze.

Before I know it, his other hand has the knife in it and one cut tears through my blouse, baring my chest.

He replaces the knife and commands, "Look." His grip on my hair turns my head back down to waist level. I see a thick, stiff bulge in his tight trousers, and I try to look back at his face to say mutely: Please, don't do this, not here.

But he keeps my head lowered, staring at the out-lined image under the cloth. And now I'm glad I'm kneeling, because my legs are turning to water as I remember what he can do to me with nothing more than his body.

I have no way to look around, but I can hear the sound of the crowd change as they notice the strange scene beginning to take place in their midst.

"Who am I?" he asks, and I start to shake visibly because this is the beginning of our ritual, and he is doing this in public for all to see.

My voice comes out louder than I expected, and I realize all around us now is silent, watching. "Knife."

A very, very slight smile, little more than a wry twitch, moves his face for a moment. Next question.

"Who are you?"

This is the hard part, and I feel myself going crimson as I struggle to get the words out. Softly. Afraid.

"Sheath."

I've said the right word, but the smile is gone again. How far is this going to go?

"Receive me, then."

No, no, but my fingers are already working on his trousers. The words, the actions, the feelings are too strong to be fought. He grasps my head in both hands and the moment my hands pull his erection free, he brings my mouth forward onto him as his hips thrust towards me. All I can think of now is how juicy he tastes, and the texture of his fleshy cock rubs against my lips and tongue.

He is still hard when he pulls away and yanks on the braid to bring me upwards, trades hands to turn me in place, and then pushes me to bend me over in front of him. Facing away from him, I can see everyone who has stopped to stare at us now; even for somewhere as undisciplined as Back Spaceport, this is not a normal occurrence, and they are enjoying the free show.

I close my eyes, but their faces remain, watching me squirm as he plunges into me not his warm cock, but a blade of cold, hard metal that makes me scream in fear and want as it slides into me.

As he twists it inside me, back and forth, side to side, the blade turning from cold steel to burning hot in what seems an instant, I cry out as I come and juice runs down between my thighs. I don't know if it's blood or just my own wet, but I don't stop to look, I start stumbling back towards safety the moment he lets go of my hair.

And the last thing I hear, as I turn the corner and fumble desperately with the handle to the closet, is Knife's hard voice cutting through the excited buzz.

"She got what she came for. Let her go—or you'll have to deal with me."

Inside the airlock, I strip off the clothes quickly and check my thighs. The gold paint which decorated my genitals has run nearly down to my knees, but there is no blood. And I recall again the change of hands that let him use the dull, left-hand knife.

I clean up as best I can in the airlock and let myself out. The temple is silent as I pass through it, pale and empty, like a ghost. The rest of my day passes in a daze; I take the treadways home, the maid helps me dress in a green kimono embroidered with red flowers, the hairdresser disciplines my wavy hair into a sleek French bun (only a few wisps of hair escape onto my neck), and the electric car delivers me to Mr. Inoue's house precisely on time.

My poise is all on the outside, though, as I step out onto the oystershell gravel of the driveway. My insides are torn in a way that does not show. What does he think of me? I ask the lowered lights of evening.

They do not know, any more than I do. What will he think if I come back, after today? For even if we return to the old ritual, things have changed: I will always know he is capable of more.

But perhaps there is no returning. Perhaps next week, I will go to Kumiko's on Friday, and she will shake her head as I look at the curtain. And I will never know why; I will only know the silent cut of goodbye.

This much is clear to me now: one pattern has ended even as a new one is beginning. So I lift my head and walk forward to the house.

When I don my silk slippers in the entrance, I feel a set of eyes fixed upon me. I look up, startled, and for a moment I am back in Spaceport again, about to begin that long walk towards Knife. The resemblance between them is that close.

But the man standing at the other end of the hall, staring at me with hard, dark eyes, has no scar under his eye. Charles pops his blond head around the corner and seeing me, makes an inaudible comment to the other man, who nods. They wait for me to come to them. I walk, and I walk, and I walk, and finally, I arrive.

"Mr. Inoue, this is Tamara, my wife."

Even up close, the similarity does not dissolve. We both bow respectfully and murmur, "Pleased to meet you."

There is nothing in his expression to say we have met before. And yet, it is exactly that which makes me think: this is him. It must be. This is how he would act. This is what he would be.

Our host moves to greet another guest, and I whisper to Charles, "Since when did a 'Riki get a last name like Inoue?"

He blinks. "Didn't I tell you that? He was adopted by one of the previous company presidents. He used to be head of a rival 'Riki company and I think they found it was easier to bring him in than fight him."

"I see." I don't know yet what I see, but I do know I see something.

Charles introduces me to the other guests I do not already know, and then excuses himself for a moment to talk business with one. I know my duties as a good company spouse, and I mingle for a while, quiet, respectful, in my place.

Then I am at the buffet, choosing among the peaches, when Mr. Inoue appears at my elbow.

"Please. Allow me," he says, and he takes the knife from my hand and cuts into the ripest fruit.

"Thank you, Inoue-san."

Nothing out of place in his face, everything correct, measured and polite. No reason for me to think he was anything other than what he seemed, one of the rare, completely assimilated Riki one sometimes finds living in the Nihi zone.

But I know. And he knows.

He places the skinned, sectioned, pitted peach on my

plate, and remarks, "Until your husband mentioned it yesterday, I was unaware that we both used the services of the numeri Kumiko. She was able to assist with your arrangements today, then?"

I nod. "Hai, that is so."

"Of course, since it was she who recommended that you and your husband be invited, she knew quite well what arrangements had to be made, even before you did."

Well before I did, I think in amusement, as I nod again. "I have always been quite satisfied by the arrangements of Kumiko in the past, Inoue-san."

"Ah, then we are both very fortunate! For so have I," he replies in the same neutral tone he has kept during our entire conversation. Not a word, not a hair, out of place, as Charles joins us and we all walk towards the dinner table together. "And I trust it will continue so," he adds as he motions for us to sit next to him.

"As do we," I smile, and look at my husband, who smiles back.

Day Journey, With Stories
Jason Rubis

I see you standing at the station, waiting for the steamer. It pulls in moments later in a blaze of shifting chrome panels, hot white clouds spouting from its head and sides. Steamers have fascinated me since I was a girl; my cousin Joselle told me once that they ran not primarily on steam, but the combined labour of dozens of slaves kept toiling away somewhere deep in the steamers' bowels. She described the slaves trudging away on gigantic treadmills, their bodies hung with bright chains, or strapped screaming to the inner walls while silver cables robbed their bodies of some form of energy necessary for the steamers' maintenance. "Think of that, Alie! All those poor slaves! All just so people like your papa can get to the City everyday...."

Even now, when I take the steamers into the City practically every day myself, I remember Joselle's stories. The basic design of the steamers hasn't changed much, as much as the People in Charge have nattered on about "streamlining" and the virtues of sleek and smooth over ponderous bulk. Of course, nothing much else has changed in the world either in, what now? Five hundred years? A few useful inventions, some stylistic development, then...stasis for another century. I suppose it's comforting, in a way. The steamers are still huge, they still have plenty of room for hidden chambers filled with Joselle's slaves. Now and then I tap my shoe-soles on the carriage floor, just as I did during those infrequent rides in my girlhood. I used to wonder if the slaves below could hear me, and think I was sending them some sort of code—a false message of hope and rescue. I could see them in their secret chambers, straining their sad, beautiful faces upwards, wondering if that day would be the day of their liberation. The cruelty of it frightened and thrilled me.

You've met Joselle; now that she's married she's become properly demure, but when we were both in school she terrorized and delighted me with tales of exotic tortures practiced in far-off (and wholly fictitious) countries. Her favorite characters for these stories were a Prince and Princess, twins, both gorgeous and quite, quite evil.

"What would they do to me if they caught me?" I would ask, trembling. It was a ritual question; I asked it during each of her visits, and Joselle invented a new delight for me each time.

"If they caught a sweet thing like you, well, first they'd make her take off her shoes and stockings. And it'd be no good crying; they're quite ruthless. Then they'd make you sit on a bench in front of a wall with two holes in it, perfectly sized to your ankles. They'd make you put your feet—your bare feet—through the holes, and then they'd lock sort of manacles around your ankles, so you couldn't withdraw them. Then they'd start the torture."

Joselle would stop there to help herself to an apple or a sweet from a bowl on the table and bite into it. You remarked on Joselle's mouth after you met her; it's still a rather pretty, cruel mouth, but then it held an absolutely hypnotic power over me. I'd squirm and watch my cousin's lips with wide eyes, not daring to prompt her, any more than I would have hurried an actual torturer. I was savouring every moment.

"The Princess would have come to sit beside you while the Prince disappeared through a door in the wall. She would inform you that the Prince's menagerie was on the other side of that wall, and that he kept all sorts of ferocious animals in it, all of them roaming free without cages. They'd been brought up from birth to trust him, obey his every command, she'd tell you, but they'd kill anyone else in the wink of an eye."

I couldn't suppress a little cry at that. I'd clench my toes up tightly inside their shoes, imagining them protruding helplessly from the wall, attracting the attention of the Prince's horrible, hungry pets. Joselle would inflict a particularly long silence then, enjoying my nervousness.

"What kinds of animals, exactly?" I'd ask timidly.

"Various species, but all of them ferocious! Wolves and tigers, chiefly. But what would happen next is that you'd feel a long, rough tongue scraping up and down your soles."

"It would tickle," I'd moan, clutching at the rug.

"Yes, tickle horribly," Joselle gloated. "You see—and the Princess would explain this to you as you sat there— the Prince had brought an animal of some sort, most probably a tiger, over to your feet and though the beast was mad with hunger, commanded it to lick your feet rather than simply bite them off at the ankles. But this was a specially trained tiger that would go mad with killing frenzy at the sound of... human... laughter."

"The wall," I said desperately. "The wall would muffle the noise."

"At that point you'd hear something sliding: a small window opening up in the wall just above your head. Any sound you made could easily be heard by the tiger."

"I would bite my lip," I continued bravely. "I wouldn't laugh. I'm not ticklish."

Joselle would reach over then and begin walking her long fingers up my arm. "The Princess would start doing this," she said. "And this" With her other hand she'd take a pinch of her long brown hair and tickle my face with it while I gasped and pursed my lips.

"The Prince would have the tiger lick only one foot at a time," Joselle told me, eyes glimmering. "Leaving another foot free for him to tickle with a long, stiff feather. Up and down the sole, between your toes. How long could you take it, Alie? That feather...and the Princess' fingers...and the tiger's whiskers and tongue, its wet breath on your poor little bare feet, tickling, tickling..."

I'd have to jump up and run up to the lavatory then, and relieve myself. I'd want badly to continue the story when I came back down, but I was too embarassed and Joselle never offered. Besides, there'd be another story next time she came to visit.

No, you'd never imagine Joselle to be capable of that kind of thing now.

You're far enough ahead of me on the platform to make calling out to you impractical, or certainly in poor taste. But I can see you moving towards the same car as me, even though a fair distance will separate our seats. So I content myself simply with climbing aboard and finding a good seat. If you are going to see me, you will see me.

Moments later the steamer pulls out of the station with a wonderful, great roar. I slide my identification card into the slot on my armrest, holding my breath until it clicks APPROVED and releases the card. I don't know what would happen if it were not APPROVED. I've never seen anyone DENIED, and assuming the possibility even exists (ours is such an orderly society), why do they allow us to wait until the steamer is on its way before we use our cards? It's a mystery to me. I, of course, used to fantasize that if my card were DENIED I would be hustled off to the steamer's depths to join Joselle's slaves in a life of desperation and painful toil. In a sense, that very nearly did happen; do you remember the article I wrote years ago that dared make critical remarks about overpopulation of the City, the way everyone has flocked to the Outer Towns and Suburbs? The politicos hated that. If some of my father's old friends hadn't proved so fond of me, I may well have been taken away in actuality. I doubt I would have found prison as romantic as I found the idea of the slaves.

At any rate, here I am, your prim Alie, my little journey begun. I tuck my identification back into my purse and give myself a few idle moments to look around the car. You're too far behind me to glimpse without swiveling my neck around, so I content myself with my immediate neighbors: businessmen and businesswomen properly attired like myself, and several young people wearing their ridiculous, voguish costumes. A boy across the aisle from me sits with his shoes propped up insolently on the seat next to him. His face is painted and his hair coloured and feathered outrageously. He pouts and taps a tune on the window—some music only he can hear. A pretty boy. He fascinates me; it wasn't that long ago I was his age, though of course I was always sweet and well-spoken. As I take out my notes and writer, I wonder whether he would pout and smirk quite so smugly if he found his hands suddenly, magically bound behind his back and if I, sauntering over and seating myself beside him, began kissing him and tweaking the nipples he displays through his artfully ripped shirt. Perhaps I would take a pin from my hair and begin pricking him very lightly about the chest and groin. What's the matter, darling? Why are you crying? Don't you like being mine, belonging only to me, to Aunt Alie? Don't cry, can't you see no one on the car can hear you?

They're all reading and looking out the windows. But I'll treat you so nicely.

Joselle and I did something similar to another boy once, a simple boy who worked in my father's gardens. We lured him to the house with sweets and bound him to a chair, he all stupid with fear of these pretty, rich girls, the girls laughing breathless and excited and perhaps a touch frightened themselves. Joselle bent close to me, and her lips wet my ears: "You're the Princess now, Alie. And he's your prisoner. What'll you do to him?"

Of course this was a challenge of sorts; Joselle wanted to see what her little cousin was made of. I wanted to impress her, but I also felt very warm, almost giddy, looking at the gardener boy as he sat panting and staring at me. I took a pin and stuck it into his arm, just above where the rope pressed his skin down in a neat line. "Come on," I whispered to him, "tell me your secrets. You have to tell me. I'm the Princess." I stuck him again and he began to cry in a loud, blubbering voice. When we let him go eventually, we made him promise never to tell anyone what we'd done, and though he gave us that promise readily, I spent many hours sick with terror that my father would confront me one day with my crime. Joselle, of course, never worried for an instant, and in fact the boy disappeared soon after. We simply never saw him again, and when I asked Joselle what she thought happened, she said "Ran away, I expect," into her coffee with a perfect lack of concern. "Unless the real Princess carried him off," she added, lifting her eyes to smile nastily at me.

That was not long ago, but long enough ago to make it hardly worth remembering. I tell myself that I have no time for such reminiscences. I thumb the writer on like a good girl and begin arranging my notes for an article I'm preparing on the restoration of a City monument. Perhaps I sit a little stiffly, absolutely erect, hoping you'll notice my hat (you did buy it for me, after all) and come to me, say hello.

I'm distracted again when a girl emerges from the door at the car's far end and struts up to my fantasy's seat, kicks his feet aside and throws herself down beside him. Her own feet are bare, and when she lifts them to prop her heels on the facing seats, I can see her soles have been intricately tattooed with zig-zag patterns. I look at her; she's even younger and more arrogant-looking than he is, her clothes even more torn and disreputable. Her hair is long, straight and blond. Her eyes meet mine and I smile. She sneers.

"Did that hurt?" I ask, leaning forward slightly. "The marks on your feet?"

"What, these?" she wriggles her toes. "Not hardly. They said they would, but I didn't feel a thing." Such a brave girl.

"I'll bet it tickled," I said, smiling. "I bet they had to strap you down for it while you giggled and giggled." Such teasing familiarities... if I were to make a direct overture to this girl, I could be arrested, such things being decidedly illegal. But the pout on her face gives me considerably more pleasure than the lawmakers could imagine. The boy smirks and she silences him with a glare.

"They use needles, not feathers," she informs me loftily. "And I'm not ticklish. I've been walking barefoot all my life. My feet are like leather."

Her feet are like silk, I thought, looking at them. Soft and white. Spoiled, silly girl, throwing her shoes away in response to some idiotic new fad. She probably stuffed them into the lavatory wastebin just now. As for the tattooing, I'm sure she shrieked and squeaked through the whole ordeal. Needles and ink and blood; I'm sure it was painful, perhaps the only pain she's ever really had to endure. But I like relating her to Joselle's stories; I enjoy imagining the Princess using a quill to scratch the strange patterns on her soles while she giggles and pleads.

I give her a placating smile and go back to my writer. But I've made her nervous, and she's taking it out on her boyfriend, snarling at him for nothing and punching his arm.

Between these two and your unseen presence, I can't concentrate on my writing. It's only minutes now until we reach the first City station anyway, so I put my things away and look out the window, admiring the sunlight glaring on the fields and houses that multiply slowly as we draw nearer to the station.

The City: stone arcs and metal towers, people and people and people. But none of them, not one, your equal. Do you know what I love to remember most? The night we spent in this very City, with you adoring my lips and learning my unfamiliar parts, my geography. The circumstances were so intimate; your heart beating against my shoulders, your mouth nuzzling them, giving me such gentle bites. We had girls from one of the better Houses come in and bind us one on another, then tease our bodies with mourningstones and feathers, tongues and nails and scourges while we gasped and struggled into each other. We were both swollen, both in desire to the point of pain, the philters we had taken staving off and then prolonging orgasm. Do you remember? Do you remember the telepath girl I had specifically requested, because of her storytelling abilities as much as her mental gifts? Do you remember how she teased you with stories that exploited the most secret, delicious corners of your imagination? The boy raped by a woman with eight spidery legs? The woman tied and lowered into a pit of eels? I think she must have liked you. She played with you far more fervently than she did me while she told her stories. I only felt the stroke of her mind on mine briefly, but then I so rarely hide my fantasies; my imagination has none of the enticing coyness yours does. My strangeness and desires are right there on my mind's surface, like colored oil on water. Joselle—the story-girl's predecessor in some ways—brought them up years ago, and they've never sunk back down into my hidden depths.

When you came you screamed, a scream that died away to a slow weeping. I followed you soon after and then we were discreetly unbound and left in one another's arms. That night is my favorite story. I wish I could find a way to tell it to Joselle, but perhaps you would find that indiscreet?

The steamer slows and shrieks and once again exhales clouds as it pulls into the City station. I collect my things and sigh and stand up. The girl is watching me sulkily, arms folded, still wriggling her toes (now rather like an angry cat twitching its tail). Excitement at your presence makes me reckless: I smile sweetly and mouth a kiss at her. It's a risk... no one is watching, but she could call me out, have me arrested and put in chains for real this time, make great trouble for me and you. But though she starts at first her face softens almost immediately and a smile of her own breaks through her sulk, making her unexpectedly gorgeous. I know she's collecting herself to return the kiss, but I turn away (relieved, I'll admit that) and begin walking determinedly up the aisle to you. Always the tease, as Joselle used to say of me. A passive sadist, she called me once, and I rushed to the dictionary.

My heart is beating hard as I approach your seat. Your head is bent over your own writer. Other passengers shoulder past me, I clear my throat, and when you look up at me, things shift, change you into someone else. A line of throat, a lifted eyebrow. You're not you now. You are Someone Else. You are my mistake. An easy mistake, due to hair color, taste in clothing, approximate height.

My stuttered apology is delivered and the you who is not you gets up and smiles and leaves the car.

Disappointment. The possibilities I hadn't known I'd been counting on pour from my eyes: drinks, reminiscences, a walk, another night in this City...re-kindled fires? All of that now gone. And I must walk in not-your footsteps out the train to a cold office and words I never cared about.

But a hand hits my shoulder and when I turn around my blonde girl and her friend are standing behind me. They both incline towards me just slightly and then both deliver obviously rehearsed, remunerative kiss to the air in front of my face. They stand smirking triumphantly, adorably.

I am delighted. I take their hands and tell them I'm going to buy them coffee. The morning is young, they are young, I am not old, and suddenly I believe again that there are new stories to be made.

Thief of Dreams
Raven Kaldera

It's dusk outside my tiny apartment, and prime time is just beginning in Sexland. I check my listings, download a list into my brain—complete with addresses and personal kinks—and swoop like a bird of prey through the dreams of thousands of people crowded into this huge, stifling city.

Interesting metaphor that, a bird of prey. I didn't actually see one until I was thirteen and rented a nature VR—something fuzzy and static-filled from the local school library about the Southwest—and there he was, a hawk, diving implacably onto the tiny mice of the desert, fate on wings. I think it was then that I decided to become a predator. It seemed the only option that could give me more than a shell of a life.

So my sig is Dreamhawk, and even if the cops knew about me, which they don't, I've left such a twisted trail around the Worldnet that they would never be able to find me. I'm the best there is, better than the Mysters or the Motleys or even Damballah. After all, I have so much more time on my hands.

(You were supposed to hear an ironic twist to those last words, in case your program is cheap and doesn't have those upgrades. After all, I can only assume someone will eventually, at some future date long after my malformed heart has given out, read these diaries and put them into VR format. Pity I can't sell the rights while I'm still alive. People always love a decent villain.)

Number one on tonight's list: Shira MacKenzie, 322 Terrace Road, age 46, who has rented "Torments of the Damned" from Candy's VRama. It's an easy one to step into; I've used it before. Let's see...Miss Mackenzie is a relative newcomer to the city, but she's rented sexvids before, all heterosex, all kinky, all bottom-space. Is she female herself in Sexland, or does she see herself as a boy? Ah, yes, female like her driver's license. Not that I care. Well... I get to play big hulking male Top tonight, it seems. Yummy, yummy.

I slip her code with ease, insert my virus program— invading her cheap antivirals is like surfing past slow-motion morons—and enter the world of her fantasy. I'm suddenly in a body, tall and muscled, dressed in scanty leather and sporting a huge erection. The scenery around me is an abandoned warehouse. I know the script of this flick well enough to know what I can and can't get away with. "On your knees, slut!" I roar. First things first. Change the hideous dialogue and lukewarm acting.

She cringes. In Sexland she's tiny, with a perfect seventeen-year-old body and fluffy brunette do. In reality she's probably dumpy, middle-aged, and graying, but hell, it doesn't matter here. I grab her by the bouffant and throw her to the floor. Then I twiddle with the program and ropes come snaking out of nowhere, snaking around her. One coils around her breasts in a figure-eight, tightening until they stand out like taut drums. Others knot themselves about her ankles, wrists, and the crease between her dimpled knees and rounded calves. Another spirals around her waist, loop after loop, cinching into a rope corset that brings her body to impossible dimensions. As a final fillip, her wrists are brought up between her shoulder blades and bound to the ropes encircling her rib cage. She gasps and cries out for help, for mercy, writhing in the throes of delicious fear and arousal.

Oh yes, there's one other little thing I forgot about. Her safe word. It would be listed in the VR's entry program, to stop the vid on command. I check it, momentarily; it's "dishwasher." I erase it.

(Oh, please. Did you really think I wouldn't?)

I step forward, looming over her, and grin evilly. "Slut," I say. "Whore. You want this. You want to be beaten and ravished by me. That's why you rented this vid. So get up on those knees and suck me, and it better be good, or else."

She looks taken aback at the mention of renting the VR. This was not what she had in mind, and it puts a notch in her fantasy. I yank her up by the fluffy hair, force her mouth open, and start fucking it. This particular Top character is pretty massively endowed, and the erection seems rather permanent. She chokes and struggles, but I notice that her hips are swiveling. I come in her mouth, shooting out what seems to be a truly unreal amount of spooge down her throat, and then force her to suck my still-erect cock clean.

She's whimpering now, moaning little things like "please, master" and "no, master." I let her have her voice for now. There are better things in store, and I want to hear her scream. I hang her from a hook in the ceiling (do real abandoned warehouses actually have all these hard points, I wonder? I've never been in one. Of course, I've never been outside my apartment in eight years) and produce several whips. Not the tacky things provided by the program; I have my own virtual set brought in with the virus. Including one rather terrifying one with six-foot tails interlaced with tiny shuriken.

She sees them and screams. "No! This is just supposed to be a bondage vid.... I don't do pain!"

"Then what good are you?" I leer, and select a cat. It lashes across her bound breasts and she screams louder. One, two, one, two, in a neat figure eight. Red welts are coming up beautifully on the artificial skin.

"Dishwasher!" she screams. To her horror, nothing happens except that I change whips and begin to lay into her ass with a different cat, this one braided with small knots. "Dishwasher... oh god, dishwasher," she moans, trailing off into sobs. My erection is still hard and I stroke it, watching her.

I decide to take pity on her. It's not that hard. I invoke my extremely illegal sexual response program and plug it into her set. It keeps her turned on, restimulates the pleasure centers so that a wave of sexual ecstasy accompanies each wave of pain. You could really fuck up somebody's natural responses with this baby. Of course, we'll only use it the one time. I can see in her face that it's working; her moans take on a different quality and she thrusts her ass out for me to work on. Somewhere in the middle of the whipping, she comes—once, then twice.

The ropes on her legs retwine so that her ankles can be spread wide apart. I produce clamps and decorate her with them. Breasts, ass, inner thighs, labia. Then I whip them off, all but the ones on the labia. Those I leave on while I bend her over and fuck her cunt, first with my cock and then with the spiked whip handle. She's coming now, again and again, in a nonstop feedback circuit. Better finish this up now before she gets brain damage. I put her back on her knees and piss in her mouth, a little fillip I add on a whim. "Drink it, slut," I order. "Remember me. You're going to jerk off to me for the rest of your life." And you'll probably never see me again. I have too many other fish to fry.

I create a temporary malfunction in the feeder circuits of her set. She'll find herself, gasping and half-conscious, back in her own living room while I retract my Dreamhawk virus and fly out to catch other prey.

Prey number two: Ms. Jaye Harper. Age 26, 6171 Fleet Avenue number 44, renting "Biker Boys." An all-male video? Yes, and she's costumed for the occasion in the body of a skinny boy™ punk. I check her past rentals, looking for the flags I know mean kinky sexvids. (I can get access to the rental lists of every VR store in town in a millisecond.) OK, she's a dyke from the look of it; this must be an experimental foray into the world of boys. No problem.

I'm waiting in the men's room of a leather bar. How cliche. I'm huge and hulking again, with an even more ridiculous cock, almost cartoonish. Boys will be boys. The leathers this time are covering, chaps and jacket and harness and Muir cap, and I smell like I haven't bathed in two days. Handcuffs and a large ring of keys jangle from the left side of my studded belt.

The bathroom door opens and she—no, he—sidles in. Online crossdressing seems to be mostly a matter of men being women (or girls rather; you can imagine the mammoth ex-football players behind the giggly Marilyn Monroe facades). Ms. Jaye is unusual, and I like that. I disable her safeword—Janine, probably a girlfriend's name—and wait, smoking a cigarette.

The boy moves nervously into a stall, unzipping his pants and pissing. The doors on the stalls are of course all broken and don't latch. I move in behind him, hands sliding down over his ass, feeling him flinch with nervousness. Keys hanging on the right, black hanky tucked neatly into right-hand pocket with a leather cock ring snapped around it. Good. This boy's no bondage bottom. "Looking for trade, boy?" I mumble sarcastically into his ear. My hands restrain his from zipping up his jeans.

He draws in his breath. "Only if... only if it's rough trade, sir," he gulps. He presses his ass against the seam of my leather pants.

"You think you can take it, you little punk?" I snarl in his ear. He melts against me. I pinion his arms behind him and snap my handcuffs on. He doesn't resist. Then I twist one booted foot around his ankles and jerk, knocking him to his knees. His face almost goes into the toilet, but he rolls aside just in time. I put one foot on the back of his neck and force his face down onto the other boot, leaning against the stall for balance. "Lick 'em good, you little punk. Lick 'em good and maybe I'll beat your little faggot ass." He does as he's told, and enthusiastically, too. I can feel his tongue like a gentle foot massage through the leather.

OK, so maybe he deserves a good beating. Let's see what we can do with this scene. I yank him up by the back of his T-shirt and hook the cuffs over the coathook in the stall door. Since this is unreality, we don't have to worry about safety issues and nerve damage. His ripped jeans fall down around his ankles and his little punk cock is hard. Wonder if Ms. Jaye likes having an erection. I know I thought it was cool, the day I hacked my first sexvid at fifteen. Didn't get around to trying out cunts for six months, but then I discovered they're just as good.

I go for the switchblade I know is in my pocket and click it open next to his ear. He flinches, but his breathing gets heavier. "Like that, do you?" I mutter, and proceed to shred his T-shirt off him with the blade. He moans when it accidentally touches his nipple and the slightest drop of blood pearls. I'm standing real close to him and I feel his cock rubbing desperately against my leather-covered leg. "Keep that little punk prick to yourself!" I snarl, slapping his face, and turn him around, slamming him up against the open stall door. That's when he notices the other guys in the room—all vidghosts— watching and leering. He hides his face in his arms, but is visibly aroused at having even this unalive audience.

I take off my belt, fold it in two, and snap the leather, making sure he hears it and jumps. Then I proceed to lay into his ass and back with everything I've got. He twists and moans, but stays put, stays the course. Good boy. Good girl. Of course I don't say it, since he didn't come here for niceties, but for brutality. After about a hundred strokes, he's a mass of welts from his shoulders to his knees, with a white handwidth over the kidney area. He's crying now, whimpering. I grab him by the throat and force him to look at me.

"You wanna get fucked, boy?" I hiss. "You want me up your skinny ass?"

His cock, after all of this, is still hard. "Yes, sir," he whispered, his voice cracking.

"Beg for it, punk." My hand grabs his scrotum, hard, and he cries out, but then manages to pull himself together.

"Please, sir, please fuck me," he gasps, and I throw him to his knees over the toilet and unzip my pants. His asshole is warm and tight, and prelubed. I swear, VR is so much nicer than the real world. No wonder I prefer it.

After I've come yet again I haul him out of the stall and toss him over to the other men in the bathroom. They're each equipped to do basic suck-and-fuck, according to the program, and Ms. Jaye deserves a nice gang-bang for her money. I haven't quite got the hang of inhabiting two virtual bodies at once, but I'm working on it, and once I do you can bet all hell is going to break out, honey.

When they're done with her I disappear them and take her by the hair again. I'm going to give her a special treat for taking that beating. I adjust the vid and run my virus through her system, reducing her to her ordinary VR self and me to a slightly feminized version of that big top. My cock vanishes as I bring her head close to it, replaced by labia and clitoris. She gasps, and looks up at me, and before she can wonder too much I tell her to eat me. Which she does, with tears of gratitude in her eyes.

You're wondering how I can change back and forth so easily, without disturbing a central gender identity. Ah well. Gender is all just a game to me, a mysterious set of masks I play with but can never fully understand. Like everything else that has to do with the flesh world.

You see, there was once a pretty teenage girl, like the ones I've fucked so many times in Sexland, without ever knowing what kind of flesh faces lived behind them. Only this little girl wasn't smart; no, she played around in the real world, the world of drugs and diseases and pain that can't be banished at the flick of a switch. Did some whoring, got a couple of viruses, got hooked on a few of the new designer head candies. Got pregnant.

You'd think a half-wasted flesh puppet like that would never be able to carry a pregnancy through. You'd think her pimp would have the decency to pay for a frigging twenty-credit shot of Sero-Abortine. But no. Instead she checks into a hospital and squirts out a pathetic lump of plasma. No arms, no legs, no eyes, no ears, nothing in the crotch but a pee hole. And burdened with, of all things, a genius IQ. Of course they didn't find that out until they gave me my first head plug—that's cranial interface to you dweebs—and my life opened up all around me.

Don't get me wrong, now. My life is just fine. I've got full disability pay, nurse machines to take care of that flesh lump while I get on with my life, and best of all, full uninterrupted free access to the Worldnet. Everything you can experience with in the flesh, I can experience here. And ten times more than that. I can be anyone and do anything. If I felt like interfacing with real people I could do that, too. They've offered me a brain transplant to a healthy body twice now, and twice I've turned them down. It's not just that there's a small rate of failure, which would have me dead on the operating table. It's that if I was healthy I'd lose my free access to the only world really worth having. I'd have to get a job and slog through life like all the other assholes. Is the flesh world worth it? I don't think so.

So. Enough ranting. All this has just been killing time until 2 a.m. when Kit plugs himself in. I've been looking forward to his fantasies with bated breath for weeks now, and it's really hard to get me excited about anything. But Kit is such a twisted little fuck that I think I'm beginning to love him. My heart flutters when I think about it.

Kit is a legal contract slave to a very rich corporate executive in Hyde Park. He lives to serve his beloved mistress, and is allowed all sorts of expensive and very fine equipment. He's not allowed to wear normal clothes, use the furniture, or leave the house, but she allows him the use of her first-class VR rig when she's out, in order to keep him occupied. And unbeknownst to her, he imports some fairly illegal sex vids and plays them while she's not looking. If it hadn't been for Kit's expensive tastes, I would never have gone beyond corner-store fantasies.

I surf into Mistress Katherine's system. Her antivirals are excruciating; they took me nearly a month to carve a channel through. I slide in through my special back door, plug into his VR system, and wait with bated breath. As soon as the vid goes into the slot, I'm occupying one of the two main characters. There are never more than two main characters, and Kit gets to insert appearances as he chooses.

I've been this persona before, and I know it well. Tall, dark-haired, stunning, legs that go on forever, and slightly Hispanic facial features. I'm wearing a sleek skinsuit of metallic silver latex. Kit likes latex a lot. Tall, thigh-high latex boots of a matching color, with a knife tucked into them. A whip dangles at the side of the big chunky belt, and on the other side a coil of silky braided copper rope is made into a carefully coiled noose.

I know whose face I wear. It's a slightly idealized version of his owner, Katherine. He's himself, his own sweet kinky self. Every hair on his body is permanently depilated except for the soft cap of black locks, and he's tattooed with floating Oriental drawings, clouds and cranes and blowing butterflies. He did a year of estrogen therapy at her suggestion, just enough to grow pretty little breasts on his slender, boyish frame; they are pierced, like his cock, with gold rings.

He's always himself in these flicks. I guess who he is really is so way out that he doesn't need to be anyone else. These vids, though, aren't really about who he is so much as what he wants. What his darling mistress will never give him.

The secret, you see, is in his fantasy.

Kit is into snuff. He likes to end every one of these nasty little vids dead in the middle of an orgasm. OK, so no one really dies in them; the interface is just cut off automatically, leaving you shaking and panting on the floor. I know, I tried one once. Not my thing, but Kit has an absolute passion for them. He's "died" at my hands a dozen times. His mistress would have a litter of puppies if she knew he was doing this, and with her image as well. Such a secret we have, my darling. I'll keep it well, never fear. I have a vested interest.

(Ah, you say, that's okay, it's only a vid? Nobody really dies? Not bad enough to be illicit? Consider then, for a moment: how do you think they are made, initially? Where do you think the neuroprogramming of death during orgasm came from, hmm?)

I walk toward him, slowly, as if I'm stalking him. He is, as usual, kneeling on the floor, not looking at me. I watch his little tattooed tits heave with anticipation. He wants it bad, this ultimate come.

I stoop and lift his chin with my hand, and he lifts his long-lashed eyes hesitantly. We've dispensed with the roleplaying by this time. I wonder if he has any idea that I exist. "Speak," I say to me. "Tell me what you want."

"Hurt me, Mistress," he says in a whisper. "Hurt me until you can't hurt me any more."

I pull the noose from my belt and loop it around his neck, like a leash. "Come, child," I say, and lead him across he room. We're in Mistress Katherine's dungeon, which is pretty lush as dungeons go. Equipment-heavy. I decide I want to be outside and I run a couple of programs to change the scene. Walls melt like running water and are replaced with bright blue sky, cloudless and intense. Golden sands stretch out around us. Bare trees crown the hill we are standing on. A hawk wheels, cries out, vanishes over the horizons. This is Dreamhawk's secret territory. I wish I could tell him how much of myself I am showing him by bringing him here for this communion, how much of a privilege it is.

There are gloves on my hands, metal gauntlets. They are for handling the barbed wire I'm going to tie him to the tallest tree with. He screams, cries out as it bites into his flesh, but does not resist. Thin trickles of blood run down over his beautiful tattoos like a web of red threads. I tie the noose to a limb, taut enough to inhibit breathing, but not enough to suffocate. My special programs are ready, held in my mind like a poker player lovingly arranges his fan of cards. "Do you love me, my beauty, my sweetness, my precious treasure?" I croon to him, stroking his face with the gauntlet.

"I love you, Mistress, oh I love you," he gasps. Music to my ears. Until I started coming into Kit's vids, no one ever told me that they loved me. I can mentally edit out the fact that he's saying it to his mistress' face.

I slap him, hard, with the metal glove, rocking him into his barbed bonds, and he screams. "Say it again," I command.

"I love you!" he shrieks, tears running down his face, one side of which is now bruised and purpling. "I love you. You are my goddess. Please, Mistress, please take me home!"

I shuck the gauntlets and remove the knotted latex whip from my belt. It hisses through the air and splats against a tree limb, and he quivers like a harpstring. Then I begin the lashing.

Kit doesn't take a beating quietly or stoically. Not for him the game of clenched teeth and rocklike stance. He abandons himself to it, moaning, screaming, begging me for mercy, begging me never to stop. I whip him until he is a mass of welts, until his tattoos stand out like repousse work on an ancient stucco wall, painted with the delicate trickles of blood form the barbed wire. The stigmata of sacred perversion, all over.

His cock is hard, thrusting vainly into the air. I stop for a moment and touch it, stroke it, feeling it throb. I want to climb on it, ride him and use it like Kali squatting over Shiva as I have done in the past, but not this time. A selection of small needles appear in my hand, and I thrust one through the tiny fold of loose skin just under the head. He arches back and sobs. Another an inch below it, and another, and another.

Now the finale. The copper rope tightens about his throat, cutting his air off, and I bring my arm back, whip at the ready. The strands will tear out the needles, the asphyxia will heighten the sensation, and Kit will come on the pain as he always does, feeling the counterfeit death in the middle of it. He will—*Shit! What the hell*— The program flickers and shuts off, sparks explode before my eyes, and the last thing I'm aware of before dark encloses me is the grinding pain than must have been the jack ripped bodily out of my head....

I'm coming to, now, slowly. It looks a little blurred. The focus must be off. Probably a bad interface. I'm staring up at a ceiling, and my head hurts abominably. White. Acoustically tiled, like a hospital. Did something go wrong with me medically? Did a nurse machine pull my plug? Was that illegal vid wormed with traps? Theories rotate lazily in my mind. Obviously I've been drugged; that fuzzy feeling is reminiscent of anesthesia.

There are two voices conversing next to me, male and female. Female one sounds strangely familiar, but out of the millions of voices I've heard I can't place it. Sounds have an echoing, unclear feel. Will somebody please fix the video and audio on this damn interface? I hate having to make do with lousy equipment. And I'm tired of staring at a vid of some white room.

"All right," comes the man's voice, nearer to me this time. "Let's get him upright." I feel myself assisted to a sitting position by two sets of hands. Are my voluntary motions disconnected? No, I can lift my head, and move my hands, but it's so hard, it takes such an effort. "He's all yours now, Kate," the voice says again. "Let me know if that monitor shows anything unusual. He's had a week to heal, and Sclepivine has speeded the process up nicely."

"Thank you again, John," says the woman's voice, firm and in command. "And I appreciate you helping in a matter of such... discretion."

"Not at all. It's been quite interesting." What the hell are they talking about? The fuzziness is wearing off, but it's still such an effort to speak. "And a way to discharge my debt to you that will be of some good use to society. Good luck, Kate."

Just as my vision is clearing, he leaves the room. The woman though, steps in front of me, and I recognize her with a shock. It's Mistress Katherine. Not her idealized face, but a more careworn version, with a few strands of grey in her hair. She is staring at me coldly, wearing white scrubs, and I can smell her perfume. The room around me is familiar, and yet unfamiliar. It's hung with chains, and eyebolts. The locked door opposite the open one is studded, like a dungeon. Bad set, I think. I could have designed better.

That's when I realize it. The interface isn't bad. It's gone. I'm looking out through real eyes for the first time.

Pure terror and despair rock me. I watch her watching me with grim amusement and realize that I have no idea how not to show everything I feel on my face. I try to speak. Such an effort! "What have you done with me!" I grate out.

"Given you exactly what you deserve, you disgusting little creature," she says in her cool voice. She is beautiful, even now. I can see why Kit worshipped her.

I panic. "Look," I say in desperation, "it was all just fun, breaking into your system. I only did it to play with Kit. I promise I won't ever touch—"

"It's too late for that." She cuts me off. "I have a few questions to ask you, and you will answer. I guarantee that." Her voice is frozen iron. "How long had you been playing snuff games with my Kit?"

I figure I'd better be honest. "About two months. Three or four times a week. Look, it was no big deal—"

Her expression tightens and she slaps me. Hard. I almost fall off the cot I'm propped up on, and only her grip on my hospital gown saves me. She hauls me up and slaps me again. I've never experienced deliberate bodily pain before and I am speechless, gasping. "Speak only when you are spoken to, and then only answer the question," she snarls. "Why did you do it?"

Okay, I'm pissed now. This I'm not going to answer, even if I had one. "Fuck you!" I snarl back.

She does something to me, lower down, and I scream. The pain makes sparks come out in front of my eyes, and there's no way I can stop it. I can't control anything here. Then she lets go, and I fall forward, gasping, wiping tears clumsily out of my eyes. I've never had to deal with tears before.

"Don't, please—" I whisper. "I'm sorry, I won't— Look, just ask Kit. He'll tell you. I never did anything to him that he didn't want—I—just ask him, okay?" I sniffle.

"I wish I could." Her voice is hard. "Kit is dead."

It strikes me beneath the solar plexus like a battering ram. "What? But the.... It was just a vid—"

Katherine's eyes are hard, uncompromising. "He killed himself two weeks ago. Asphyxiation, in his room. There was no vid involved. I was home, and he didn't dare log in." She pauses, and then stabs it in. "I suppose he was trying to recreate your special treatment. Perhaps he'd gotten used to it."

Tears are blinding me now. Oh, Kit, Kit, my precious sweetheart, you little idiot! Why didn't you wait for me? Why didn't you leave this woman for me? But of course, he never knew I existed, never knew how much I loved him. He'd never leave his mistress for a ghost in the machine. Gone. All gone.

Katherine takes a seat, waits until I'm done. I wipe my face on the bedsheet. The helplessness of this body is frustrating. "How did you find me?" I ask softly.

"I ran his programs to find out what he'd been doing, and I found those vids. Then I checked my guards, and discovered I'd been invaded, many times, by a very clever and careful probe. So I used some vids of Kit inserted into the snuff to lure you, make you think he was still there. Then it was just a matter of waiting for you to take the bait, and tracing your probe."

I realized that the last time we'd played, when I'd showed him my secret place, he'd already been dead. And I never knew. Only a bloodless vid with the mind of this cold spider woman behind it, waiting to pounce, hunting the hunter. Kit, my first real love, was dead to me forever.

I blew my nose on the sheet, and that's when I notice my arms. The wrists are tattooed, delicately, with Oriental butterflies. I look at my chest, knowing with terrible clarity what I'll see. Swirls of green and blue float on the small breasts, around the gold rings. "No!" I scream, and launch myself at her.

I'm not used to the clumsiness and effort of a body, and I only succeed in falling off the bed with a thump, tangled in the sheet. "You bitch!" I sob. "You won't get away with this! It's isn't legal! I didn't give consent!"

I hear her voice above me, unmoved. "A surgeon I knew owed me a favor. And you, you're a danger to society. I'm doing them a favor, too, getting you off the Worldnet. Besides, who will know? Kit's still legally my slave. You signed a contract. I can do anything I want with you for another year and a half. Then, well, we'll see. Oh, by the way, I've permanently removed your link."

I put a hand up, feel the shaved head and the healing sutures where Kit's sweet brain came out and my twisted one went in. "But I can't—I'm not—like him, I—" I shut up. I've lost. Will I go mad, I wonder, before she takes her full revenge? My whole world, lost. My power, stolen. I feel her looming over me. Funny how presences have so much more—well—*presence* here. I refuse to look up, rocking back and forth on the bed.

"I could have turned you in to the cops," she said. "They'd have taken it out, too, but then you'd have spent your life inside a nursing home with no sensory input, going crazy inside your own head."

She has a point, but I stare stonily ahead.

"Do you want it back?" she asks. "Your link, I mean."

My head jerks up, but I still do not meet her eyes. Do I? What do you think, you bitch?

"Depending on your behavior over the next year and a half, I might be convinced to... well, we'll see how much you want it. How much it's worth to you."

I smile ironically and meet her eyes, finally. Does she think I'm going to fall for that? I'm not a submissive. "No," I say. "You'll never do that. I know you too well. Remember," I point out, before she can protest, "I've been you. Frequently."

She glares, and our gazes thrust at each other, like fencing foils. In that moment I swear to myself that she will never break me, never. It would be a betrayal to Kit, who died for me. Then she smiles, a terrible smile, that of the adversary. "I'll leave you for a little while," she says. "You still need to heal up some more before you start your... work here. Oh, and there's a holo box in the corner. In case you want to watch it." I watch as she turns and leaves, locking me in.

I am in mourning, and I wear the skin of my dead lover on my back, like a penance. So she wants revenge, I think. I can beat this. After all, I'm Dreamhawk. Mistress Katherine doesn't know what a dangerous creature she's locked up in here, what cunning and guile live in this twisted brain. She hates me now, but that will change. I know—better than Kit—what makes a sadist love you.

And that's the first thing I'll have to do. To make her love me. And then use her to escape.

I'm Dreamhawk. I'm up to any challenge.

Color of Pain, Shade of Pleasure
Renee M. Charles

Without even needing to see the face—so artfully covered by the sharkskin-covered brank—I immediately knew that the woman who knelt before me had to be Orlina La Roux. Her neck was secured to the stainless steel whipping post by a velvet-padded joug whose long, snaking chain was draped lightly across her welt-streaked bare white back. This was Orlina of the insatiable appetite for pain, and still more pain, of the most exquisitely exotic sort. While her hair alone might have been a giveaway (so luxuriously thick, so richly highlighted with strands of glistening gold among the henna and russet), it was the sight of that fine-fleshed, creamy pale back, with its remaining deep pink shadows of former welt-marks that was unmistakable. Had I not placed each of those criss-crossing blemishes there myself?

Yet, she was already writhing in place with anticipation of my latest laying-on of the knot and spike-ended thin-curling whips, even as I languidly cracked the flailing strands against the doorway, to shake off the excess water from their over-night soak (what liquid does to the leather can be excruciatingly pleasurable). As I approached her, the spiked heels and small rounded toe-pads of my shoes clicking on the polished white tile like finger-snaps, I saw Orlina's small, taut-nippled breasts rise and fall in rhythm with her sharply accentuated breaths.

My most frequent customer obviously couldn't wait for the stinging caress of my dripping whip, so, of course, I made her wait all the longer for that sinuous, if brief, embrace. From its usual spot on my table of tactile toys, I picked up the small, brush-like device (which I'd fashioned myself), affectionately dubbed "The Teaser" by some of my more verbal customers, and I gently tapped the business end of the brush against my open palm. The Teaser was studded with dozens of nettle-fine spiked balls, each loosely attached to the cured-oak base, and I reflexively winced before saying "Have we been waiting long—as if I couldn't see that you want it," and giving her the first disciplinary swacks of the Teaser across her rounded bare bottom, then following that with lighter, but nonetheless steady smacks of the instrument on her bowed shoulders, the sides of her jutting breasts, her taut thighs, even the top of her closely-sheared mons.

And with each stinging kiss of the Teaser, her wide grey eyes would glisten momentarily with the crystal shimmer of unshed tears, even as her pupils dilated with unmistakable pleasure, then contracted when the last fleshy echo of the pain died down. And between the secure straps of the brank, which held the molded-cock-shaped insert deep in her mouth and prevented her from crying out or even speaking, I could see her lips purse against the tight-pressing straps, as if she were kissing the very air with each downward arc of the Teaser.

Once her milky-light skin was mottled, ruddy pinkish-mauve, I lifted her up by the strap attached to the outside of her brank, and motioned for her to grasp the smooth, tall sleekness of the whipping post until the top of her skull was touching the post and spread her legs for balance. I told her "You haven't squirmed nearly enough.

I want to hear you moan behind that prick between your teeth. I need to hear you beg for more and more until my arm burns from within... you filthy little slut. The sight of you sickens me, you groveling, simpering pasty bitch. You need to bleed a little—"

And, true to our thrice-weekly (at the least) scenario, Orlina began writhing in place against the post, whimpering behind the stubby penile gag, and grasping the chrome pole before her claw-like, anxious fingers... until the first whistling arc of the knot-ended thongs slapped against her flesh. She jerked forward, even as she then arched her back toward me, anticipating the next stinging swipe of my mane of soaked leather and tightly-knotted tips. With each criss-crossing, branding slap of my whip, she let out deeper and throatier moans of unmistakable pleasure, such an intense, orgasmic noise I felt myself grow slippery-damp along my shaven, leather-encased crotch. As the first razor-fine welts began to run dribbling red across her shoulders and upper ribcage, I let my eyes wander upward, to where her hands grasped the pole... for safewords aren't so easy to hear through a brank's mouth-filling insert, but hand-signals are quite easy to catch, provided one doesn't get too carried away.

But tonight (or what passed for night on this space-station's ever-circling rotation around the moon), Orlina's right hand didn't form her usual "OK" sign (thumb and forefinger in a circle, other fingers splayed out stiffly) of submission and retreat. The thread-fine dribbles of blood coursed down her silky-fine flesh in DNA-spirals, dripping runnels which pooled slightly at the curving swell of her melon-like buttocks. I wondered if, in my own state of sexual arousal, I'd somehow missed the signal to stop. The "rules" for each encounter were implicit, rather than explicit—no mistress or master was to stop whatever s/he was doing to a client unless the "safe" word or signal was given, so, short of flaying a customer to death (and given our advanced technology, even death can be a most temporary thing), none of us usually stopped unless our own hearts seized up from the effort of inflicting that desired pain/pleasure on our demanding customers.

Orlina La Roux's blood now ran across the rounded curves of her buttocks, and into the crack between her pink-mottled cheeks, and still there was no indication for me to stop my leathery pummeling of her now cross-hatched back.

"You've punished me, little wretch," I lied, as I loudly massaged my leather-encased upper arm, before closing the distance between us in three snapping strides and unfastening her brank, then all but ripping it from her head. When her face was turned in my direction, her mouth was wrinkled in a moue of disappointment, and her eyes—initially unfocused with a haze of pain/pleasure—soon were fixed on me with a steely blaze of anger.

"I didn't give you the signal," she hissed through her even, pale ecru teeth. "I didn't see all the colors, all the new shapes—" before placing an open-palmed hand across her mouth, and backing as far away from me as the chain securing the joug around her neck to the pole would allow.

I stopped massaging my arm long enough to ask, "Colors? Shapes? Is there something going on that I've been... missing?" Having been a Space Services Mistress for almost ten years, I didn't think that there was any S/M or B/D practice—or resulting gratification—I hadn't already experienced.

La Roux stood with her head bowed, so that her russet mane slid over her blushing face like opaque curtains. I gathered up bunches of her hair in each hand, and yanked them aside to reveal her pale oval of a face, admonishing her, "Now, now, no secrets from your mistress... I do all, and I have to know all."

"The colors... the ones I see when you inflict pain on me. Different ones for each type of torture... and when it gets intense, the colors, they're... they're incredible. Almost unworldly, like galaxies intermingling... so much more intense than just an ordinary orgasm—"

Curling her hanks of hair around my hands, so that they formed huge curls of either side of her flushed, but wan face, I said, "Oh, like what you see when you press the orbs of your eyes, and those patterns of light and color form on your inner eyelids—"

Shaking her head (albeit slightly, under the pressure of my hands pinning back her hair), she insisted "No, not at all. These are colors hovering right before my face, like a veil of moving, shifting color. Then, when the pleasure hits me, the colors take on different shapes, forms I can actually feel pressing against my cheeks, my lips, my nose. The shapes, they grow more varied with each new expression of pain... but I need to keep it going long enough to remember what I'm seeing and feeling—"

I loosened my grip on her hair as realization set in for me: Orlina La Roux was blessed with synesthesia, able, through a sensory mix-up, to mingle heretofore seemingly incompatible sensory impressions into something new, something tantalizingly pleasurable. In fact, one of the other mistresses who worked the Sex Shop here on the station could "taste" colors (she claimed that the sight of blood was sweeter than chocolate), but the implications of being able to see one's own pleasure and pain were intoxicatingly heady, even for a person as sated by mock-sadism and jaded by the sight of writhing, panting "slaves" as I'd become over the years.

And the sight of Orlina's visually-aided orgasms did make me wet at the core.

Picking up the slack of her joug-chain, I wound the linked coil of metal around my left hand, while my right tightened around the handle of my whip—and the sparkle of anticipation in my client's eyes brought a sweet glow of pleasure to my already musk-slippery labia. I gave the whip a quick wrist-flick and slapped the knotted ends against Orlina La Roux's thighs and knees, before asking "Why do you need to remember each new colored shape of pleasure? You're not keeping secrets from me, are you... slut?"

Wiggling with suppressed pleasure at my taunting pet name (I wondered briefly if the pain of being called filthy, degrading names also produced those elusive visual light and color shows for her), she again hung her head, this time biting on her lower lip to keep from answering me... and eliciting another swipe of the whip, this time across her gently concave belly and henna-haired mons.

I could actually see her labia jerk in time with the hard kisses of the whip-ends, and when I looked up into her eyes, they were again wide-pupiled and awash with the glimmer of unshed, sparkling tears.

Holding the whip before her eyes, I whispered harshly "Either you tell me what you're seeing, or no more of this"—I shook the dangling tendrils of the whip for emphasis—"either from me, or any of the other masters here. I need to feed on your pleasure, even as I dole out what you need."

"I'm very hungry for it, Mistress Serilda," she whispered, eyes lowered, her voice husky with suppressed desire. "I've been bad, and I need for you to punish me—"

Ignoring her typical slave-prattle, that masochist's lament I'd already heard (in surprisingly few variations!) thousands of times before, I reached out and knuckle-clamped one wrinkled nipple—gently, though—and continued. "Your pleasure from my inflicted pain is essential to me now, but there's no pleasure for me in just watching you squirm and grovel; I need to know what each smack of the knotted thong reveals in your sight, to feel those... shapes which caress your flesh. And I must know why you need to remember each new mingling of color and shape and sensation. Is it for your pleasure in your bed each night? For the times when my whip, my Teaser, are still and unused? For those moments when your flesh still longs for discipline, for the harsh caress of my dripping, flaying embrace? Do not turn your head, I have not commanded it—"

Obediently, even meekly, Orlina La Roux's head of rippling red-gold turned toward me, but her eyes were wide-pupiled, as if gazing upon that which I could never directly see—and it was then that a hunger grew in me to share in that unique, synesthesia-enhanced worldview, even if by proxy.

Using the master-key attached to my chain-link and leather-tab belt, I detached the chain from her velvet-and-metal collar and led my slave-for-the-evening toward the wall of the chamber studded with hanging-loops. Upon these various leather-and-latex garments hung, all unisex, with easily adjustable hook-and-loop closures (after all, the crew and support staff of the Station come in many sizes and sexes... too many for even the storeroom in the S/M shop to carry individual gear for each person who might want or need it!). Glancing from the cowering-and-loving-it Miss La Roux to the selection of rubber and leatherwear in her general size range (small-boned and creamily nubile), I finally selected a "hoop" body harness. The harness featured lightly-spiked breast hoops, the ends not much sharper than a little finger-tip, but still stimulating and a network of body straps which culminated in a between-the-legs thong dotted with raised, shining chrome studs.

I ordered her to don it, then helped to cinch it tight against her flesh so that the surrounding skin bloomed around each strap and criss-crossing thong, her pert, upturned breasts were mashed tightly against her ribcage and her nipples strained behind the spiked hoops. I turned my attention to her wrists and thin, shapely ankles, this time choosing latex gloves with attached wrist cuffs and loops for adding a lock or a chain, plus a pair of spike-heeled patent-leather shoes whose ankle straps could be linked to form an effective pair of ankle-cuffs.

After she was properly cinched and bound and confined, I hooked a finger through the thin, studded thong which ran through her labia, and half-dragged, half-pulled her to the restraining wall of the chamber, where the leather-and-plush-pile Chevalet stood, along with hoods mounted on the wall for suspending wrists or ankles in various configurations, a punishment chair which jutted out from the wall, and a variety of hanging ropes, chains and straps sturdy enough to suspend a well-bound and eagerly willing slave.

Since I'd already paid ample attention to her back and shoulders, I decided that if Miss La Roux wanted to see her colors and shapes of pain/pleasure, she'd have to endure some attention to her exposed privates... and no mouth guard or brank this time, no matter how much she seemed to crave it.

After all, I was going to get a little something out of this night's session, too.

I arranged her supine on the punishment chair, her upper back and mid-section on the smooth-worn wood-and-metal, her buttocks flat against the wall, her belly rippled in at the navel. I then pulled each of her legs up and out, attaching the ankle straps to the wall, so that she was spread-eagled in a wide, welcoming "V," pussy up and exposed around the confining studded strap. Once her legs were secured, I locked her wrists together under the extended tongue of the chair so that her flattened breasts were aimed at the ceiling, while her head lolled off the end of the wide, flat chair bottom.

"Can we move...? I didn't think so," I hissed through smile-clenched teeth, while flicking the whip against her pinioned thighs and calves. "But I know my tender little slattern can talk, can't she now? And she must tell her mistress everything she sees—"

Staring off at a point where the ceiling met the far wall, Orlina whispered, her voice thick with ecstasy. "Every flick of the whip is magenta, tinged with dusky rose... little revolving triangles of magenta... merging into tall, pointy pyramids when the orgasm hits... ma-magenta, and the brush of rose—"

Closing my eyes for a second, I could almost see what she described; the tantalizingly sharp triangles and pyramids floating and shifting, leaving a haze of deep purplish-red in their wake. But surely, there had to be more—

Click-stepping toward my table of sex-punishment toys, I scooped up a handful of them, then hurried back to where my slave for the night was splayed in all her pink-and-cream glory. The staccato hail of my heels echoed in the smooth-walled and -floored room. Since my job includes humiliation as well as domination of my slave, I turned my attention to the trimmed patch of slightly curling hair between Orlina's extended, cuffed legs, and the moist folds and wrinkles of the inner labia within. First, I picked up a well-spiked and nubbed latex tickler, which I slipped over an oval love egg. After pulling aside the thong which had straddled the length of her slit, I pushed the tickler-covered vibrating egg into her waiting, slightly gaping vagina, asking "And what does this new sensation look like—what color is each tickling now inside you?"

Arching her pelvis toward me, until her lower back was well off the surface of the chair, she moaned. "Tiny amethystine circles, chains and ropes and weaving strands of them, encircling my face, pressing against my cheeks, my chin... beautiful blue, dozens of—"

Her voice broke off when she heard the buzzing whine of the small battery-powered wet/dry clippers, but as soon as the chiseled tip of the vibrating blade touched the top of her mons, clearing away her curls to reveal silky blanched flesh below, she added, her voice barely recognizable for all her panting and gasping "Ovals... ovals now, darkening to sapphirine, pushing against my face, my neck, my breasts... circles into ovals, green-blue into darker blue... all over me, pressing, caressing...."

As I sheared her lower labia, letting the vibrating body of the shaver rest against the puckered inner labia and also-vibrating love egg within her, my slave Miss La Roux's utterances became too punctuated with groans of pleasure to be understood. So, once her tender, juicy folds and smooth curving spots were free of hair, I used a long plumed feather to whisp away the remaining clippings. And as I slowly, carefully brushed the downy wand-like end of the feather against Orlina's denuded, pink-dappled mons, she whispered between groans of gasping, panting orgasm, "Gold... golden-bright squares, all pointy angular ends pressing into me, revolving, shifting, pressing down all bright and shining... too bright, too—" She squeezed her eyes shut against the brilliance of her individual vision, before her labia began to jerk spasmodically and clear bubbles of musky juices welled in her glistening pinkness.

(For perhaps the first time, I longed to break the unspoken rule that no mistress or master shall have actual sex with a slave, but had to content myself with jerking out the love-egg by its cord, and merely watching the reflexive ripple of her flesh as it gave up the studded, jiggling sex-toy with a soft, kiss-like parting-of-the-flesh noise.)

Realizing that my disciple's expression was perhaps a little too enraptured, too caught up in unvarnished pleasure without the attendant pain she usually craved, I picked up a pair of chain-joined nipple clamps, and—using both hands—simultaneously affixed them to her upturned, spike-encircled nipples.

"Ohhh—emerald, bright emerald cones... points all digging into my face, my neck, in my ears... all green, all—"

Closing my eyes, I could "see" and feel what she described, and the intensity of it was staggering, but there were so many other toys and implements in the room, and so many more colors and shapes to experience before our session would come to an end.

When the bong-like tone which signaled the end of our evening's session sounded, both of us jerked visibly, rudely intruding upon our mutual (albeit somewhat one-sided as far as actual experience went) give and take of pain-color and shape-pleasure. With much reluctance, I undid her legs and arms, and helped her off the chair. As she unfastened her restrictive garments, I clung to my role of the evening as I asked/ordered her "Every other session we have will include what you see and feel... just as you will give me the satisfaction of knowing why remembering each new mingling of your synesthesia and my ministrations is so crucial to you."

Totally nude now, Orlina stood before me head bowed slightly, and replied "You will have your satisfaction very soon... next week, in Section S, at the showing there. When you come there, you will understand why your touch upon my willing flesh is so urgent to my needs," then hurried past me, out the slaves-only door, and into the waiting dressing area beyond.

And, since masters and mistresses are forbidden to follow their fleshly conquests into that area, I was unable to administer a reprimand with a quick flick of my whip-bearing hand. But as I watched her bright-striped back and buttocks vanish from my sight, I could almost feel those revolving, sharp-tipped triangles of magenta-seeping-into-rose....

The compliant Miss La Roux did not come back to my chamber of punishment and pleasure for almost a week, and although there were other willing bodies who awaited the hard caress of my whip, my Teaser, and who most eagerly allowed me to bestow upon them the whims of imagination, leather and confining latex, I found myself longing for the sight of Orlina's waving tresses peeking out from under the bindings of her brank, or the mottled stippling of her fine-pored flesh. And during those days, my whip came down harder on the waiting expanses of flesh, and my individualized sex-torments grew far more intrusive, far more exquisitely intricate, until my slaves for the evening began saying or signing their safewords far earlier than was their usual wont.

Being paid by the hour, I soon felt the pinch of my unusual excesses, for my allotment of pay credits was lower than usual... so much lower, that I was forced to forgo my own for-a-fee session of pain-sex with one of my fellow mistresses (the icy showers followed by insertion of dildos warmed to well above body temperature, or the "massage" of synthetic nettles on my uncorseted spots), and instead had to seek out the more inexpensive amusements offered to the Space Station crew as a whole—

—amusements which included the ever-changing show of crew-created works of art and artifice in Section

S, the art show I'd never before had the time (or tolerance for enduring such a lack of stimuli) to attend.

Feeling almost alien in my non-usual, standard-issue crew uniform (I wasn't even able to wear my corset or harness under its clinging confines), I morosely drifted from wall of bad art to display case of even worse art, until I noticed a group of tightly-packed, obviously enraptured crew members standing in front of a series of eerily-lit objects on a low-slung pedestal.

My six-inch heels were forbidden in the rest of the station, which featured soft-tread floors in case of sudden zero-g conditions, so I needed to stand on tip-toe to see over the shoulders of the shortest of the crew members surrounding the items exhibited. All I could initially make out was intense pockets of neon-bright colors... magenta, brilliant blue-green into evening-blue, golden-yellow, and finally an intense emerald-green which was almost too powerful to gaze upon.

But the colors were obscured in spots, by the outlines of hands... moving hands, which belonged to the crew members who stood closest to the display, and who tentatively caressed and prodded the glowing, amorphous works of art—

When you come there, you will understand why your touch upon my willing flesh is so urgent to my needs.

Craning my neck forward, until the pain of straining my muscles sent shivers of near-orgasm through me, I squinted my eyes slightly, in order to better see what rested beneath that highly pigmented luminosity. In each case, the stylized, achingly mobile suggestion of a nude female was either curled or splayed or resting supine on the unyielding hardness of a white-tile base, each with an almost featureless oval face and deftly under-defined nakedness. And each one was covered with glowing geometric shapes which seemed to hover just above her contorted curves and lean lengths of leg and arm. With a gentle touch of the person viewing the sculpture, each bright-tinged shape came into squishingly-soft contact with the female beneath them, pressing into that synthetic flesh just enough to partially vanish in those creamy, semi-translucent depths, so that the "skin" of each sculpture became momentarily suffused with that same intense blooming color, so that "woman" and "shape" and "color" were merged into a unified, blissfully integrated whole.

And while each sculpted ovate face remained basically unchanged, the resulting interactive interplay between viewer and what was viewed revealed heretofore unseen curves and hollows on the face, so that each orgasm of shape and color in turn awakened the viewer to that which had been previously unseen, unappreciated, in each small female configuration. It was impossible to tell whether the source of each color's brilliant illumination came from within or without each separate hovering "shape," but judging by the expressions of blissed-out ecstasy and abandon on the faces of those who caressed each statue, it really didn't matter where the light came from, for there was heat enough for all who either touched or merely witnessed each construction's sensual transformation.

I needed to summon all my previously untapped stores of patience before the crowd around the display cleared enough for me to approach one of the radiant artifices, but as soon as my fingertips made contact with those floating magenta-rose triangles, the rush of tingling, aching, throbbing, smarting delectation was almost too much to bear while standing clothed and ostensibly decorous in a public place. And when I closed my eyes, I literally felt the nudging and mindless pushing of the whirling triangles against my flesh, accompanied by the radiant close-by glow of the magenta color-fire within each ever-shifting pointed shape.

And with each new sculpture I rubbed and gently fingered, I again felt/saw mixtures of color and shape which spanked and thrashed my very essence far more completely that any well-wet-and-knotted whip or sharp-spined Teaser could ever have done. The juxtaposition of previously uncombined sensations was more intense, more bracing, than even cooling-but-still-warm wax dribbled on my soaked-cold wet flesh.

Only when the last of the interactive models had been explored and tactilely savored could I numbly wander away from the display table, eyes lowered like the most submissive slave before a thousand-tendrils-thick whip, barely able to walk upright on the springy, slightly oozing floor beneath my feet. Then a cool, firm hand grabbed my upper arm, steadying me, so that I could finally look upward, like the mistress I usually was—

—straight into the dancing-from-within bright eyes of Orlina La Roux, who was almost unrecognizable when clothed in the standard station uniform, with her rippling blaze of hair bound in a neat, asexual bun at the nape of her thin neck, and a badge emblazoned with her name and job description (Computer Programmer, Bio-Neural Unit) pinned to her slightly heaving lapel.

She glanced to the spot behind me where a new group of Station crew members were busily interacting with the tableau of sensory delights, before whispering "Did you notice the name-card on the table? I hope it is sufficient to satisfy your demand of me, my Mistress—"

That Orlina had created the works of artistic ravishment resting on that table had been clear to me upon my first glimpse of them. Surely I didn't need to see her name there to know her work, but Orlina grabbed one of my hands, and gently, reverently, steered me back to that luminous display, toward the open end of the long table, where no one was standing, and where a neat rectangle of lucite was embossed with the following inscription:

COLOR OF PAIN, SHADE OF PLEASURE

BY

"MISS" ORLINA LA ROUX

AND

"MISTRESS" SERILDA LURLINE

I found myself actually blushing when I read the dual credit on that shining rectangle, but managed to forestall further embarrassment by biting down hard on my tongue before facing Orlina once again, this time demurring. "I'm flattered, but I hardly deserve such credit. I was only performing a paid service, servant to your fee, just as you were servant to my whims and orders—"

"But I can hardly inflict the necessary pain on myself, without forgoing the pleasure of being suitably bound and restrained, now can I," she countered, with suitably subservient downward-glance of her eyes, before adding with a shade more eagerness "The gallery has promised me another table for the next new show, provided I can create even better, more stimulating works of art. But for one with my condition, there is only one constant perception, one set of shapes and colors, per particular stimuli. For me, the stinging kiss of the whip will always be magenta, and so on—"

"But with the experiences of a new stimuli, you'll experience a fresh mixture of shape and shade, no?" I asked, while envisioning her dappled pink-white flesh submerged part-way in icy water, just before the dripping descent of the slightly-cooled wax... or the excruciatingly intense expression on her face as I used piercing tongs to lift and pull tender, soft protrusions on her body... As if she could somehow read my expression (as if my body had become one of her interactive lighted sculptures), Miss Orlina respectfully lowered her thick-lashed eyes, and begged "I know I've been very bad, very disobedient in the past, but with the suitable chastening and penalties, I know I'll please you, and earn your satisfaction."

Leaning in close to her, so that no stray pair of ears might hear my reply, I whispered, while imagining the meaty feel of the whip handle—or the heated length of the burning candle—in my palm, "Only as long as I get first crack at the finished sculptures... in private, so I can wear my usual gear while enjoying them, and I must witness you partaking of them, as well. In my chambers, where I keep my personal store of implements and toys. And many, many candles—"

"Ones that drip easily?" she asked, and as she uttered those words, I mentally reminded myself to make sure that the next time I could afford a session with one of the Sex Shop mistresses, that I beg her to castigate me until I could stop showing my desires so plainly on my face.

Being party to an artistic process is one matter, but showing personal gratification to one's slaves can ruin the whole S/M experience. Make the slaves too soft, too easily let off—

"By the way, Miss Orlina. The next time, you create your... pieces, make sure my name goes first on the placard," I demanded, and her bow and nod of acceptance—reluctant acceptance—was like music to my eyes.

Jane
Lauren P. Burka

I.

The pet shop man looked up when the door opened. "Hey, Jane," he said.

"Hello," said the parrot on the counter.

"Hey," she answered.

"Can I get you anything today? Some nice goldfish and a bowl, perhaps?"

"Hello," interjected the parrot.

"No. Just looking. As always."

The parrot said, "Pretty boy."

The gray old man waggled his finger. "Mind your manners. Jane's not a boy." The parrot tried to nip his finger.

"It's an easy mistake," Jane said. She was long and lank with buzzed-short hair and an angular face. A belt pouch lay over her crotch like a man's bulge. Her black jeans and stained leather jacket hung wet on her frame, giving her the look of a butch junior mechanic.

"Such a sweet thing as you? You should be in pictures, not filming them."

"Hello," said the parrot helpfully.

Jane considered telling him that she had once won a pissing contest, for distance. But the pet shop man lived in the same fantasy world as most of the pre-war folks. Women, to him, were ladies.

She stopped to look at the rat cages. Pink-eyed, white-furred rodents slept in a heap in their food dish. Most of them were snake food. Jane used to own rats. She had treated them with meticulous care, but they still died just after turning three years old. Which was longer than most relationships lasted, she thought. One of the ferrets recognized her and rattled its cage until she took it out and held it.

"Row, row, row your boat," sang the pet shop man to the parrot.

"Hello."

"Gently down the stream."

"Hello."

Sighing, the man turned on the radio instead. The parrot picked up a pen and chewed on the end.

The ferret climbed onto Jane's shoulder and nested against the back of her neck, its pink-nosed face looking out under her ear.

"You should get a pet," said the man, over the sound of the game. "You look lonely. Pretty girls shouldn't be lonely."

"Hello."

"I'm not lonely," she said, uncoiling the ferret and returning it to the cage. "I just like holding them."

"And I wish you would take the bus. The Avenue is not safe at night."

"I'll be fine."

"See you tomorrow night?"

"Sure."

"Hello."

It still rained in thin drizzles. The gutters were full, clogged, slicked with oily rainbows. Jane splashed through, wet to the ankles of her workman's boots, her collar turned up to her ears.

The Avenue wasn't dangerous. Its broken facades housed the addicted, the anti-social, and the criminally depressed. Police swept the Avenue a couple of times a year, usually after a citizen strayed too far out and got mugged. Avenue-dwellers fancied themselves outlaws, not realizing (or not admitting) that they were the zoo. Dangerous people were always culled.

Jane liked to walk down the Avenue just before dark. Someone at Authority probably knew this. But Jane was a Trusted one, and must be allowed to get away with some things.

Wet stones loomed out of the rain curtains. The granite-slab pavement under her boots had frozen in a tortured convulsion, cracked around a collapsed sewer. Some doorways were lit with flickering, greasy flames that spit at the weather. In one of them two young men were talking. Their hair was cut and colored; their clothes displayed odd-colored patches and rips, disguised as style. Jane stopped, her hands in her pockets, and watched them. Their conversation died, and they turned to look at her with black-shadowed eyes.

Apparently it wasn't that cold out. Neither of them made a move towards her, and she shrugged and went on. After she passed from sight, the two hustlers held each other in a way that had nothing to do with sex.

The drizzle gave way to a downpour.

Jane watched the people moving in and out of the rain. Most of them were young. Some of them talked to themselves. A teenage girl held a faded blue stuffed bear by a fire set in an old stone planter while another girl tried to get her to eat something burned on the end of a stick.

Someone was pacing Jane. She could hear the soft splash of his footsteps in the full gutter. Jane slowed her pace and felt for the thin knife up her jacket seam.

"Alms, sir. Alms for your unfortunate brother."

Jane wiped rain from her eyes. "There's an alms-house up the other side of the Avenue," she said.

"I know that."

The speaker was shorter than Jane, with longer hair. He was dressed in black, or perhaps he was just wet.

"So what are you doing in the rain begging change from honest folk?"

"You tell me."

Jane flipped a lighter from her pocket. In the yellow glow the kid (for he was a kid) blinked china-blue eyes and wiped his nose on a sleeve. He wore a leather jacket, but the arms were too short. Silver ribbons in his braided hair sparkled. Jane realized he wasn't as young as she thought. Everyone else on the Avenue just looked too old.

"You looking for a bit of trade?" she asked.

He shrugged. "Food. A bath. Maybe a scratch for my itch."

"What's your itch?"

"Heroin."

Jane whistled. "Where'd you come from that you could get it? Nevermind. All I've got is medical-grade morph." She turned and walked away.

"Wait." He was running. "What do you want for the morph?"

"More than I'll get from your skinny ass."

"I'm good for it. Whatever you like. Please?"

Jane smiled to herself. She hadn't even hit him and he was begging.

They had come to the end of the Avenue. Most of the streetlights worked in the kinder part of town. A patrol car floated past. The man behind the wheel waved at her. The boy flinched.

"You got a license to be selling your ass?" asked Jane.

"You know I don't."

"You're dirty meat," she said. "I should call the cops. They'll let me watch while they work you over."

"You won't."

He was right, of course. She'd have to punish him for that.

Jane lived four blocks down on a side street. She unlocked the front door and let the boy walk in before her. Water leaked down one wall and puddled in front of the stairs. Their footsteps echoed on the hard walls. Metal railings wobbled at their touch.

"Stop here," said Jane.

They were on a landing with nothing but a broken bottle and bare stone walls where the plaster had come down.

"Here?"

"I want to see what you're good for before I let you drip on my carpet."

He glanced to either side. In the hallway lights his face was perfect, almost sculptured, colored white and pink from the cold, framed by black and silver hair. There were rings in his right ear. "We'll be seen."

Jane could have told him that the only other residents were a married couple on the third floor, who were on vacation, and old Ms. Evans, who was half-deaf and lame and had her groceries delivered. Instead she pinned him against the wall with one sharp hip against his crotch.

"Shut up," she said. "You move when I tell you and be still otherwise."

He squirmed. She slapped him, her wet hand numb to the impact on his cheek. He hissed, his heart beating hard enough to hear, the sticky sweet smell of his body stronger than the stairways's other reeks.

"Bastard!" he spat.

Jane smiled. "You said you would do what I want."

"I am doing what you want." He smiled back and arched his spine, rubbing his cock on her leg. "You're still a bastard."

Interesting.

"What's your name?" she asked.

"Morgan. Yours?"

"Jane."

"Sure it is. Hey, are you a girl?"

"Yes. Why do you care?"

"I should have called you a bitch instead."

She slapped him again.

Morgan spat.

Jane got both his hands in one of hers and pinned them up over his head. Her other hand opened his belt and then his jeans. His cock was warm and dry but for the wetness at the end from humping her leg. Morgan's breathing echoed in the narrow space as his sex grew hard against his belly. Jane weighed it in her hand. It was short but thick, with curly black hair matted at the base, wandering up his belly in a narrow stripe. Jane slid his belt from his jeans and doubled it, tapping his cock with the loop.

Morgan whimpered. But his eyes were open, his pupils dilated, and his legs scrambling to spread wider on the step.

"You'd like that," said Jane.

Morgan grinned, showing teeth. "Do you like me to like it?"

Instead, Jane buckled his belt around his hands and ran the end up over the railing above them. Morgan sighed, letting his arms take his weight. His eyes snapped open at the snick of Jane's knife.

"She likes me to bleed, too," he whispered. Light reflected from the blade into his eyes. "Vampire."

"No." She drew the knife along his beardless jaw, leaving a white line. The point eased downward, slow as the rainwater that still dripped from his hair. Jane snagged the neck of his shirt. The fabric parted.

"Hey," he said. "Not my clothes. Skin heals."

"I'll get you another shirt." The knife opened the faded black cloth, revealing his lean ribs, anemic-pale skin, and thin scattering of black fur. And something else. Jane opened the shirt all the way down and lifted the thin steel chain with the knife point. It was anchored on either end to rings in his nipples.

"Cute," she said, replacing the knife and taking the chain in her fingers.

"Present from a friend."

"You're pretty," she mused.

"Thanks."

Jane yanked his chain. "That wasn't for your benefit. You're pretty. You're too healthy to be a dope addict. And you have pierced tits. Barbaric custom. Authority doesn't approve. It locks people away for two years of treatment. Even the rings in your ear would lose you a job preference."

"So what? You think I'm a cop?" Morgan pumped his hips at her. His flagging cock stirred.

"No. I think you're an Islander. You made it onto the mainland before the revolt and massacres. You have no identification and no money, just an aristocrat's attitude and some unusual tastes."

"Maybe. But now I'm a whipping boy off the Avenue. And my hands are getting numb."

Jane gave the chain a last yank, released the belt, and climbed up the stairs.

Morgan yelled at her back, "You owe me fifty on top of the morph, already." When she didn't turn he trotted up after her, holding his clothes together.

Jane's door cast a square of light into the hall. She stepped aside and let Morgan enter, tripping on his pants.

"Stop," she ordered. "Strip and leave your clothes here."

The leather jacket hit the floor, followed by the ripped shirt. The jeans clanked when they fell. Morgan stood naked and shivering, but not at all subdued.

"Can I have my fix now?"

"No. Bath's to the left. Take your time. I'm making dinner."

"I'll go jerk off in the shower," he said, and left wet footprints on the blond carpet.

Jane stripped when he was gone, changing to a kimono from the closet. Her clothes went into the 'matic. His shirt went to the trash, and so did his pants after she cleaned them of the small metal things in the pockets. Lockpicks, a knife with a broken blade, coins useless since the Islands sank. There was an elastic black cord, too. His jacket and boots joined her clothes. Jane went to see about food.

The shower was set for thirty-six degrees. Morgan turned it up to forty and stepped into a warm spray of water. He folded his arms and shivered while his body temperature rose to normal. Now that he was warm it was time to be clean.

The shower dispensed a burst of soap-laden spray, and Morgan began to scrub his skin free of its surface grime. The too-intimate smell of stale, alcohol-tainted sweat went down the drain. So did long black hairs that came free when he scrubbed his scalp. A few scabs peeled away to reveal new skin.

Now that the preliminaries were over, Morgan leaned against the wall and soaped his groin. A paying client would want him clean all over, though since he hadn't eaten in two days he could skip the enema. He should wait for Jane before he climaxed. But she might just hit him a few times, sit on his face, and throw him out unsatisfied. He was, after all, playing the bad boy for her.

He melted into the soft pressures of the water and braced his legs as he worked himself to full hardness with a wet hand. Reaching back, Morgan used a soapy finger on his asshole, cleaning and pleasuring himself at once. He meant to keep it going as long as possible, but the smell of cooking food invaded the bathroom, and his stomach gave a long, appreciative growl. His grip tightened and he sprayed up into the shower.

Wrapping himself in a large towel, Morgan took Jane's comb off the counter and exited the bathroom.

She lived in a one-room dwelling with plain, comfortable furniture. The kitchen, half the room, was large enough for a table. There was no bed in sight. Morgan sat on the sofa and began combing his black and silver hair.

Jane glanced up. He was hoping she'd say something about the comb, but she turned back to the pan on the gas flame.

Morgan inhaled the smells of garlic and vegetables.

Jane spooned rice from a small pot. Morgan watched her move in the kimono. Her legs would never pass as male.

"What's for dinner?" he asked.

Jane shut the stove off and walked, barefoot, to the chest of drawers under the window. Morgan craned his neck to try to see what she was doing.

"Get down on the floor," she said. "Leave the towel."

Morgan knelt with a straight back and knees slightly parted, his white skin and black body hair sharp against the soft carpet. The older scars and newer bruises gave his body a well-used look, like his boots.

His back was tense with the effort not to turn and watch her. A soft thing wrapped around one of his wrists and pulled. He tried to flex his arm as Jane snapped the hospital restraint onto his other wrist, too tight. Morgan shifted. His bound wrists forced his chest out. The chain shivered with his breath. Jane tugged on it.

"Chicken for dinner," she said. "You're dessert, so eat well."

Morgan tried to climb to his feet, but she shoved at the back of his knee just as he caught his balance.

"Down. If you want your dinner, you crawl."

Morgan gave her a wounded look, and began an undignified squirm to the kitchen table. Jane spooned some rice and stir-fry onto a plate and set it on the floor. She took the rest to the table and began to eat, with chopsticks. He reached the plate and sat back on his haunches, scowling.

"I don't think I'm hungry."

"If you're too proud to eat like a puppy, you'll never get your dope."

Morgan lowered his face to the plate and picked up a steaming bit of chicken in his teeth.

"Good dog."

The food began to vanish in bigger mouthfuls until the plate was clean. Morgan's stomach growled again. He sighed and leaned down further to eat spilled food off the floor. Jane set a bowl of water on the floor next to the plate. Morgan drank, snorting as he got water in his nose.

Jane picked him up by the hair and wiped his face with a towel. As she cleaned his cheeks, Morgan looked up to her, relaxing into her grip with a grateful ease that approached submission. She stroked his lips with a finger.

"I'm not done with you yet."

"I know."

Jane unlinked the cuffs. "Heel," she said.

Morgan crawled after her and stayed in the middle of the carpet when she told him. In moments he might be held down screaming and cursing as he gave his body over to her attentions. He looked down at the cuffs still on his wrists. Did she have a matching set for ankles? Morgan hadn't been tied tight since...

"I want you to take your prick in your hand and stroke it for me."

Morgan blinked. He was eager, even after the knee-weakening come in the shower. Fear made it easy to get hard. So did the thought of the narcotic rush that waited for him if he pleased. He wet his fingers and spread spit over his cock head. Jane was watching him, but looked bored. He took a firmer grip and worked with his fist. Maybe he could come before she ordered him to stop. There might be some sublime punishment if he did. He got himself to the edge quickly. His cock was purple. Release coiled in his belly. She was going to order him to stop, wasn't she? This was the part where the trick teased him mercilessly, except it usually happened at the end of a session. But Jane just watched him with arched eyebrows as he came over his fingers, quietly, and lifted his hand to lick it clean.

Jane got up and opened the drawer. He watched her back and wondered if she was impressed.

She turned around and held out a white plastic rod looped back on itself with the ends stuck in a tape-wrapped pipe handle. A home-made flogging implement.

"What about it?" he asked, sounding more breath-less than he liked.

"Get your ass in the air," she said.

Morgan put his head down and his ass up, irritated that she was going to beat him after he came. It was easier to take pain when he was on edge.

The flail struck his thin haunches with a hungry snap. Morgan gasped and arched his back. His knees collapsed, hiding his red-striped ass in the carpet.

"Did that hurt?"

"Yes," he muttered, waiting for the order to present for more abuse.

But Jane was taking something else out of the drawer. Something that jingled. Morgan looked up and saw a red rubber ball roll past his nose, ringing.

"Fetch," said Jane.

Morgan got his knees under himself and crawled after the ball. The double stripe of pain on his ass faded to an almost-pleasant glow. But it hadn't been the kind of pain he liked. Too sharp and biting. Not at all like a belt or a hand. Jane was going to be a bigger challenge than the usual.

The ball had rolled to a stop against the kitchen counter. Morgan reached out to pick it up.

"Touch that ball with your hands and I'll whip you bloody."

Morgan froze and put his hand back down. She couldn't want him to carry it in his mouth.

"I'm waiting."

He crouched and took the ball in his teeth. It forced his jaw wide and made breathing difficult. The bell inside it rang. This was disgraceful.

Jane held her hand out for the ball. Morgan let it fall for her, wishing he could wipe the drool from his chin. But Jane threw the ball across the room again. Morgan looked up at her, offended. She reached for the flail. He was half-way across the room before he realized he had made the decision not to get hit.

He fetched the ball again, and she threw it. Why couldn't she use him like she had on the stairs? He could lick her until she came, or take half her fist up his ass. Why did he have to crawl like an animal?

Morgan fetched. His knees hurt. So did his wrists. He took dust in his mouth with the ball and, once, a dead insect. He halted, panting, in the middle of the floor. The ball lay under the table. Jane was on her feet with her instrument of torture. At least he was about to get some attention. Maybe she'd tie him up.

Gritting his teeth, he thrust his ass out to meet the first blow. He had no breath to scream. But the pain was a clean thing, not like the rasp of the carpet. He took it as long as he could stand, then flung himself down on his back.

Jane's kimono was coming undone, but she didn't seem to care. She lifted the flail and cracked it across Morgan's thigh. He howled and scrambled out from under her, across the floor, to the red ball. Like a good pet. When he retrieved it to her hands, he was crying for the first time in years, and the first time ever for a trick. She didn't seem to notice.

Time passed in a hell of indignities, a blood taste in his mouth, aching joints and abraded skin. The tears drained him of defiance. When he faltered, blows rained down on his tender flesh.

Until he lay still to receive her attentions, with no restraint but his own exhaustion.

Jane's skin was flushed when she lay down the flail and shed the kimono.

"Get it up for me."

Morgan reached for his limp cock. It didn't want to play, not after two orgasms and the tears. The carpet was too rough for his welted back. Jane was tapping the flail against her palm. Fear chilled Morgan's guts, but it warmed him too. He was half-hard when she straddled him and rubbed her cunt against his cock. That did it. He felt her slide down, swallowing him whole.

"You stay hard until I come."

He nodded, gaze locked with her cruel, gray eyes. He would do anything she asked so she wouldn't want to hurt him again, so that she didn't make him cry. But he didn't have to like it, just lie back and let her fuck him.

Jane came, squeezing his cock with her tight cunt, clawing his shoulders with her nails. It hurt him more than the beatings, but he was too tired to come. Too tired. Then he was alone on the floor, cold and wet and sticky.

Jane was tossing things at him. Clothes. A pair of her jeans, and a shirt. A bag with his tools and toys. His own jacket. He could see his boots sitting by the door. A roll of script hit the ground next. More than the fifty he had demanded. He should count it, but he didn't want to move. And something else.

Morgan grabbed for the disposable syringe and ripped open the package. The elastic was in the bag. He tied off his left arm and went searching for a vein. Found one. His lab-engineered neuroreceptors cheated him out of addiction, but true pleasure was rare enough to crave. Morgan needed to need something. The needle bit, giving him the sweet rush of a high-class Islander affectation, an orgasm that wouldn't fade for hours, the crutch that would make it possible for him to dress and walk down the stairs.

Jane was watching him with clinical interest.

"I'm kicking you out," she said.

Morgan started pulling on the clothes. Her jeans were too long and bagged around the ankles. The wad of script was almost too fat for the pocket. Untraceable. Food, shelter, and maybe drugs.

"Thanks," he said, smiling like an idiot.

"Next week," she said, her voice washing over him like the rain. "This time next week."

Morgan considered. He didn't have to work now, not for a long time. She had seen to it.

"Yes," he said, because he was free to consent. "I'll be there."

But Jane looked for him all up the Avenue that day, and he was nowhere to be found.

* * *

II.

The famous reporter stood still under the lights while an assistant fixed her hair and dabbed the sweat from her neck. Awed Haven staff stood clustered in the doorway. Jane was on a step ladder fixing one of the sound units.

A production manager chased the onlookers away. The News team was ready for magic.

"Good evening, Citizens," began the reporter. "Today we're visiting the Safe Haven Institutional Support Center. Safe Haven is charged with bringing street kids, many with severe health problems, into a productive relationship with our free society. The majority of inpatients are the children of brave men and women who died in the War. Recently Safe Haven has opened its doors to refugees from Floating Islands One and Three. These new patients present unique cultural adjustment challenges for the dedicated staff.

"A Haven patient will be treated for all physical and mental health deficiencies and trained in a vocation appropriate for his or her abilities. Once a patient is certified well enough to work, citizens or corporations may purchase a work contract for the cost of the patient's debt to society.

"The contract system guarantees former patients food, shelter, and continued treatment as they get back on their feet, minimizing the cost to you, the taxpayer."

In the dark behind the ranked 3-D recorders, Jane smiled to herself. Jane used to work at Haven. She knew all about the forced medication and surgery, and the lax oversight on contract workers. Jane was a Trusted one, a politically and socially tested Citizen, whom Authority charged with keeping its human zoos.

Somewhere in the sprawling Haven complex, a kid was getting bent over his cot and fucked, or written off as "untreatable" if he didn't cooperate. Lucky kids were out in two years with the memories of their stays wiped clean. Those who wouldn't break for Authority were sold off for medical experiments and, rumor had it, spare parts. But the public would see clean, white hallways with cheerful pictures, wide-eyed idealistic staff doctors, and happy, adjusted former patients.

The first time Jane took a boy and a rubber strap into a private treatment room, his tears and red-striped buttocks had aroused her more than anything else in her life except the discovery of masturbation. But after the novelty wore off, each session left her vaguely disappointed, like food without salt. Even her orgasms lacked flavor. Eventually she applied for retraining and took the News tech position.

But the first night she held a hustler pinned against the stairwell wall, she learned the difference between coercion and power. A whipping boy was a professional. He might not enjoy the work, but he had more choice than a citizen in the job lottery. When one of them crawled for her, licked her, held his asscheeks open and begged her to fuck him, she had already penetrated, subverted, and despoiled his will. That was sweeter for her than making a hardened street survivor cry like a baby.

So Jane paid them well and watched for the ones who came back again after they knew what she wanted. Most of those, like the arrogant puppy with the rings and the silver in his hair, disappeared. Now Jane was back in Haven for the day, dogged by a restless arousal that would have dampened her jeans if the hot lights and disinfectant smells had not made her slightly nauseous.

Jane wheeled a recorder into a brightly-painted room where patients were engaged in art therapy. Boys from mid to late teens painted pictures and made sculptures out of small pieces of wood. They were dressed in hospital clothes in bright, primary colors, and their hair was cropped skull-close. There was not a sharp implement to be seen in the room.

"Got anyone who looks alert?" asked the production manager. "We need a kid who doesn't drool or stagger for the interview." One of the staff doctors made a sarcastic comment, and the two started an argument.

Jane leaned back on her stool and watched the aloof reporter watching herself in a monitor. Bored, she turned to the patients. A therapist was teaching two kids to make clay pots. Other patients moved their hands in repetitive gestures, trapped in the spiral of medication. One kid was trying to sleep on the bench. A woman therapist shook him awake. He looked up, cursed at her, and turned over. The woman made a note on a clipboard and trotted out of the room. The patients closest to him edged away.

Jane leaned forward and studied the problem patient. His hair was shaved down to fuzz, but there was still a hint of silver among the black.

"Morgan," she whispered.

He sat up and stared across the room. His eyes didn't focus, but he mouthed her name.

The therapist returned with a large orderly. Morgan fell off the bench and crawled into the corner.

"This is the one that bit me," said the orderly. "I'll take good care of him for you."

The therapist watched, smiling, as the orderly strapped Morgan's wrists behind him and dragged the kid into the hall.

Jane watched him go.

"Let's forget this group," said the production manager. "Got any presentable girls? Audiences like to see girls."

* * *

"Why do people own pets?" asked Jane. "They eat and shit and we clean up after them. What do we get out of it?"

The pet man shut off the radio. A calico kitten was washing herself on the counter. She looked up when he scratched her behind the ears.

"You're talking philosophy, girl. Why don't you ask me how to cure a case of worms?"

"That's not what I need to know."

He screwed up his face with the effort of unaccustomed thought.

"Pets bring us outside of ourselves. We give them what they need, and they give us company."

"They don't talk much," said Jane. "Except for parrots who say hello."

"I don't know about that," he said, scratching the kitten. "I had an old tabby who stood in front of the fridge and said 'mewk!' when she wanted milk."

Jane grinned.

"They talk as much as people, but they don't always use their mouths," he concluded.

"Pets get old. They die."

"That's never a reason not to love someone. I was married for twenty years to a beautiful lady. She got the cholera that summer when they bombed out the sewers. But I wouldn't trade those twenty years for anything, not even hope of heaven. Now I bring home cats, and sometimes a puppy. Keeps me from getting lonely. Makes me care about something."

"Even when they're sick?"

"Even when. Pets make us better people. We have to live up to all that love."

Jane nodded. "Thanks."

"Sure you don't want anything? I got kittens. And a de-scented, neutered skunk. Friendly and clever."

Jane shook her head. "But could you do me a favor? It's kind of odd."

"Anything for you, girl."

Jane pointed to the pegboard wall of leashes and dog collars. "Can I have a leash? The black one?"

"Uh, sure." The pet man looked puzzled, but plucked the leash down from the wall with a hook-ended stick.

"Ten fifty."

Jane paid with a credit card.

"See you tomorrow?" asked the man.

"Maybe. I got work to do."

"His name is Morgan Blair-Tremain, of the First Floating Island Tremains," said the contract administrator. "He has no surviving kin but a pair of cousins who are under political asylum on New California. They have other things on their minds. We haven't treated his kind before. Current medical theory indicates that those raised in a climate of..." she wrinkled her nose, "aristocratic privilege adapt poorly to a socialist society. As for his genetic enhancements, well, he's a living violation of the Equal Birth and Opportunity amendment.

"Nevertheless, given his involved treatment and the fine for unlicensed prostitution, his current debt to society is twenty-two percent over average, so we don't foresee a favorable contract buyout for him."

"But you will consider my offer."

The administrator shrugged. "It's not unheard of, but we haven't finished his first course of treatment. We can't guarantee him safe to handle. His vocational skills are minimal. On the other hand, he is fit and healthy, with a good immune spectrum." Perfect transplant material.

She sighed with resignation. "Give me a couple of hours and I'll have a contract ready."

Jane nodded. "Before I sign, I want a few minutes with the merchandise.

The administrator pushed a button. "Is patient 18-11C presentable?" she said into a microphone. "Yes? We have an interested contractor. Please arrange an interview. A private one."

"Thank you," said Jane.

"It's our pleasure, really. Turning out healthy, responsible adults is our mission, but whenever possible, we must recoup the cost of treatment."

Jane arrived at the interview room first. Two large, ugly men arrived five minutes later dragging Morgan between them.

"Want us to sedate him, ma'am?"

"No, thank you."

One of them tossed a shock prod on the table. "Keep this, at least. And yell if you need a hand with him."

Morgan sat in the other chair when they left. His earrings were gone. A lot of him was gone.

Jane flicked the shock prod off the table.

"Morgan, do you know me?"

"Yeah. Jane. You're the cruel woman who made me eat off the floor. Hated it."

He wiped his nose, reminding Jane of that evening on the street.

"I had this cousin named Liandra," he said. "She was tall, gorgeous, strong. Father got fed up with me one day and told her to take over my education. I needed discipline, he said. She used to take me to her room every evening and whip me for every mistake I made that day. I made lots of mistakes. After a while, she would whip me when I was good, and lock me in the closet if I wasn't."

"Did she fuck you?"

"No. But she gave me the rings. She said when I was old enough to marry, she'd make sure my wife had a good tight hold on me. She pierced my cock, too, but that was just before the Revolt. I spent two weeks hiding in small boats with nothing but dirty water, and it got infected. Had to take it out."

"Morgan, why didn't you bottom out to these people? A boy who gets on his knees and sucks cock gets left alone otherwise."

"I'd rather die."

"Cause they're men?"

"No. I've done men, for money. It's cause they're pigs."

"Ah." The desire to touch him was like an itch in Jane's fingers. "I've got an offer for your consideration."

Morgan looked up. "Yeah?"

"I've got money. I was saving it for a stead in the reclaimed territories. It's a lot of money. Enough to buy out your contract. Remember how I did you last month? I'll do that again, every night, as soon as you're strong enough. But it isn't worth it to me unless you consent."

"You going to give me morph?"

"No. I want you to feel it when I hit you."

Morgan was crying without a sound. "I could say yes just to get me out of this place," he whispered. "That's not consent."

"It's not, but I know you wouldn't do that, any more than you would kneel and suck here."

"I hate you."

"Yes or no, Morgan."

"Yes."

"I didn't hear you. Louder."

"Yes, Jane. Take me home."

* * *

Jane took Morgan home in a taxi and carried him up the stairs. He was too weak even to crawl, so she stripped them both and got him into the shower. Their wet skins sliding together in the water should have been erotic. Instead Jane dried him off, rolled out the futon, and got some rope.

"What are you doing?" Morgan asked when she began trussing him to the futon.

"I know what drugs they gave you. They sent us home with a month's supply. But I won't give you morph, and I won't have you addicted to something that isn't even fun. I want you secure before you start to hallucinate."

"I won't hallucinate."

But Morgan did, all night, screaming and sweating and pissing himself, and biting Jane once when she got too close. Jane sat watching him until they both fell asleep near dawn.

The leash lay in a pile at the foot of the futon. Morgan examined it when Jane was gone at work. The black leather handle felt new and crisp, and the chain ran though his fingers until he held the snap at the end. He knew what it was for, but he pretended he didn't. Jane hadn't used him since she brought him home.

Jane waited. And the longer she waited, Morgan knew, the harder she'd use him when he was ready. So he ignored the leash until long after he was well and strong. And Jane ignored him, except to feed him from a plate on the floor and toss him a blanket when he went to sleep at her feet.

Until the night when she was reading on the couch, and Morgan couldn't stand it anymore. He took off his clothes (her clothes, jeans cut down to size) and folded them in a pile. The leash snapped around his neck. Jane didn't look up. Morgan knelt wondering what he should do next. Then he took the handle in his teeth and crawled to her.

Jane lay down the book, took the handle from him, and pulled until the chain tightened.

Morgan looked up. "Take what you paid for. Bitch."

Jane tied the leash to a couch leg and got the flail out of the drawer. Morgan covered his face with his arms and listened to his heart pound. His cock was already stirring.

The first blow across his back gave him such a release that he screamed. An hour later when his ribs and thighs were all colored with welts and he had near-choked himself with the leash, and come, twice, without permission, he was begging and praying to his goddess to send him to the hell where he belonged.

Jane shoved him down on his belly and put a foot between his shoulder blades while she got something from the drawer. Kneeling between his thighs, she spread him wider while she poured cold lube into her hand.

Morgan wailed and cringed when he felt the first chill touch between his red-striped cheeks. Jane yanked on his leash while she stroked his tight hole open with one finger, then let him breathe as she took him. His whole body went slack when she found his prostate with two fingers. Morgan pushed back against the penetration like a queen cat in heat.

Jane reached under him to pinch a ringless nipple.

"You're going to take me past the knuckles by next week, hear me?"

No answer.

Jane twisted his nipple.

"Yes, Jane!"

She wiggled her fingers. His body tensed, hips fighting to pump against her impaling hand. Jane tightened up the leash again and he came, his face near as purple as his cock.

Jane pulled her hand out and wiped it on a towel. Morgan lay flat, sucking air, in a puddle of sweat and come.

"Get up and do something useful with your mouth."

Morgan climbed to his knees and put his head under the skirt of Jane's kimono. Her cunt was wet, unshaven. He licked the thin outer lips and the fold of inner lip that poked out between them. Opening her with his tongue, he found the little hood of flesh that hid her clitoris, the deep hole of her cunt, and all the places between. Each touch made her move, swear, claw at his head. She reached down and shoved his face against her so that he was grinding his tongue right against her clit. She came. Morgan shifted to follow her as she convulsed, until Jane reached down and slapped him so hard that he fell.

Jane stretched and sighed. Morgan waited for a word of praise. When none came, he pressed his lips against her instep, once, and started to back away. Jane tugged on the leash. Morgan almost panicked when she took his chin in her hand.

But it was only for a kiss.

Morgan opened his mouth for Jane and let her do what she wanted to him, went limp when she bit his throat, and whimpered when she took him in her arms. Pleasure weakened him and made her strong.

"Get clean," she whispered, unsnapping the leash.

Morgan crawled off to the bathroom. When he returned several minutes later, soaped and rinsed, Jane had the futon unrolled on the floor. Morgan went to lie down at the food of the bed.

"No," said Jane. "In the bed with me."

"You honor me." He kissed her foot once more, he who had been a prince in a vanished land.

They lay down together for the first time in dark and in warmth.

"I love you, Jane," he whispered. "I love you."

Agent of the Free
Neal Harkness

I was not always as I am now, a time-serving bureaucrat in a forgotten colonial outpost. When the great events of our time were shaping the future of the world, I was at the center of the maelstrom. I served with honor throughout the war, winning the Order of Valor at the Battle of Smolnica, accorded more honors for my leadership during the Great Winter Offensive. I was proud to represent the forces of freedom in the battle against the ideologies of tyranny. I tell these things not to exalt myself, except in that so doing I might illustrate how far from grace the events of the war's chaotic aftermath caused me to fall.

The occupied territories were a sea of humanity. In the spring following the collapse of the Black Army, and the capitulation of its weaker allies, civilian refugees, repatriated prisoners of war, displaced persons of every imaginable description clogged the roads, sleeping in the barren fields and burnt out buildings of the defeated nation, often resorting to pillage and riot in the depths of their desperation.

It was to impose some measure of control on this seemingly overwhelming situation that the high command instituted the Strategic Camp System, to which I was assigned. It was with great reluctance that I accepted this new posting, but as was pointed out to me by my superiors, my combat skills were no longer in great demand. I supervised the mustering out of my faithful veteran troops, and reported, with no great enthusiasm, to the ironically named Camp Freedom.

The Strategic Camps were designed to be vast clearing houses of humanity, their primary purpose to sort the teeming throngs, and facilitate their relocation to their various appropriate destinations. This task, although formidable, quickly became a relatively simple bureaucratic routine, and required little of my time as Camp Commander.

It was the Strategic Camps secondary purpose that kept me occupied. In addition to the masses of innocent victims of war, the hordes which passed through the system contained other elements. Escaped mental patients and common criminals were the least of them. There were monsters on the loose that spring. The government and the Black Army had committed a multitude of atrocities, against their own people as well as in the lands they conquered. The exposition and detention of war criminals for trial was my most important personal duty, one which I freely admit I relished. Unfortunately, it necessitated an unsavory procedure, the detention of witnesses, who were more often than not, victims themselves of terrible crimes. My heart yearned to send these witnesses on their way to rebuilding their lives, but in that chaotic climate there was no way to assure that we would be able to retrieve them when the time came for their testimony.

Camp Freedom was situated near the important southern junctions, in an area that had harbored a number of major government facilities. One of the most notorious of these was the mildly named Institute for Behavioral Studies. We had heard during the war horrendous stories of the inhuman experiments that went on there, but they were in many cases so far beyond the realm of human decency that I had considered them propaganda, designed to instill our troops with loathing for the enemy. I learned the awful truth shortly after assuming command, in a briefing by my executive officer,

Captain Nevis, who had supervised the groundwork in the establishment of the camp.

The briefing took place in my private quarters, as my command office was not yet operational.

"I assure you Col. Straiton, the stories you've heard about the IBS are the tip of the iceberg." He told me, while rifling through a thick file of documents. "Neurological reprogramming, terrible experiments with aversion training, fetish implantation, purely speculative brain surgery..."

"Fetish implantation? I don't understand what you mean by that, Captain."

Nevis blushed. "Well, sir, they, it's hard for me to discuss this sir, I'm a religious man. They—"

"Take your time, Captain."

He spoke in a rush. "They took preadolescent children and used sophisticated conditioning techniques to ensure that they would develop certain, certain, well, strange sexual proclivities sir."

"They what? Why would they do that—it's just sick."

"I certainly concur, sir. According to documents we secured at the institute, they reasoned that if they could induce fetishistic desires into the general population they could, by withholding or supplying the means to indulge those desires they could better control the populace."

"That's absurd. Could such a scheme possibly work?"

"Well, sir, although they seem to have had some success with individuals in the program, they never got past the experimental stage."

I pondered Captain Nevis' information. I had been brought up in the military tradition of family, honor, discipline. Sexual depravity was beyond my purview.

"Do we have any of these so-called doctors in custody Captain?"

"No sir, the Intelligence Service is investigating reports that they were all killed when the facility was bombed in February."

"And the children?"

"Well, they aren't children any more sir, this program had gone on for some time. The five we have here are all in their early twenties."

"And what—ahem—what is wrong with the ones we have?"

Captain Nevis clearly was as embarrassed to have to answer the question as I was to ask it.

"Two of them, Svor and Polepy, are apparently, er, interested in articles of clothing made of rubber. The Knin woman is sexually aroused by receiving enemas and Zebrak, by women's feet."

"But how could the government control things like enemas and feet."

He looked at me as he would a slow student. "They were just trying to implant the, I guess you would say 'normal' fetishes, sir. If they were successful in mastering the technique, then they would have used it to make the people crave some item or service that only the government could supply."

"I see. And the fifth subject?"

"The fifth subject is the most troubling case of all. It seems the young woman, a Miss Oleska, receives sexual gratification from being subjected to various forms of corporal punishment. Whipping, flogging and such."

"My God! They could create a whole population of willing slaves!"

"Ironically, sir, one of the things they discovered, according to their files, was that the subjects implanted with a desire for punishment sought it out, and were therefore more rebellious than the others."

"Thank God we freed these people from such madness."

We moved on to other topics, but the plight of the victims of such a fiendish plot continued to disturb me. I resolved to devote particular attention to the rehabilitation of these poor souls, but in the days following my briefing with Captain Nevis, a large number of prisoners, members of the infamous Black Terror Battalion, were delivered to the camp for processing, and were by necessity, my higher priority.

I did manage to find some opportunity, in the few quiet evening hours after my daily duties had been discharged, to peruse the files on the Institute victims. The foot and rubber fetishists baffled me, and I was repelled when I read the file on Miss Knin, the enema practitioner. The file on Miss Oleska, however, was strangely compelling. I was drawn to open it nightly, trying to convince myself that it was the single haunting picture of the young woman, Staya Oleska, contained within, that drew me back. It was a head and shoulders shot, taken immediately after the liberation of the Institute. Yet, despite what must have been extremely traumatic circumstances, she had faced the camera with a confidence, one might even say a haughtiness, that was entirely at odds with the history of degradation the file's documents described. She did not possess the broad features and dull expression so common among the women of her people. Her features were sharp, her dark eyes piercing, even in the deficient field photograph. Those eyes pulled mine back to them again and again. Despite my better judgment, I knew that I would have to meet Miss Oleska, or be haunted by her.

My opportunity came shortly. The flow into the camp was waning, and at last I reached the point where I could control my own schedule. I ordered Captain Nevis to arrange an inspection of the Special Detainees Quarters, where Miss Oleska, and her compatriots were housed.

The inspection took place on a blistering hot July morning. The Special Detainees Quarters were segregated from the main body of the camp, located in a requisitioned riding school . The stables had been converted into housing for the detainees, while the century-old school itself had been appropriated for office space by the unit's staff. Captain Nevis and I entered the school and met with Major Crimond, the Intelligence Service officer who, while nominally under my command, ran his sector of the camp as a personal fiefdom.

I listened with feigned patience as Major Crimond, in between puffs on his ever present cigar, explained the purpose of the Special Detainees Quarters. Its occupants were individuals whose legal status was in doubt. The largest contingent in the unit was comprised of industrialists and profiteers who had supplied the enemy war machine. Our government had yet to determine whether to hold these individuals culpable for War Crimes or not, therefore they could neither be released, nor incarcerated in the stockade. The quarters also housed a number of other questionable types, including several family members of high ranking government officials. I asked Major Crimond why the victims of the fetish experiments had been relegated to his care.

"Primarily because we have yet to apprehend any of the Institute staff, sir, and if and when we do, we will need the testimony of these individuals in their trials."

"But we have many similar cases in the main camp, Major, why are these people segregated?"

"Well, sir, they are known perverts. And there is some feeling in the Intelligence Service that they are not so much victims as they are co-conspirators."

"I don't believe that view stands up very well, Major."

"Then sir, I suggest you come with me."

He led us out of the school and back to the stables. We entered what must have once been the stable keeper's quarters, now the duty room. A pair of regulation issue cots stood to our right as we entered, while a heavy antique desk guarded a door opposite the outside entrance. A young corporal was the only personnel on duty. He snapped to attention as we entered.

"At ease, son," Major Crimond said. "Corporal, please present detainees Zebrak and Oleska for interview."

"Yes sir." He spun on his heels and dashed from the room. We waited in awkward silence for his return. He was back momentarily.

"Detainees Zebrak and Oleska, present for interview," he reported, his voice cracking nervously. A short, belligerent looking young man, whom I recognized as Zebrak, the foot fetishist, followed him into the room. Behind Zebrak strode Miss Oleska. As she entered the room she gazed at us disdainfully. Major Crimond dismissed the young Corporal and he left the room. When the door had shut behind him, Miss Oleska slouched against it, her arms crossed over her chest in a pose of studied indifference. Her every movement was riveting. I had seen more beautiful women, but none who radiated as much sensuality. I struggled to maintain my professional bearing.

"Captain Nevis" I muttered, "Perhaps you could serve as translator..."

"We need no translator, Colonel" Zebrak snapped, his face flushed," We were raised with the finest of continental educations. I, myself speak four languages fluently. Fortunately so, since we have no one else to speak for us...."

"Yes, we all know how well your masters treated you," Major Crimond sneered.

"Colonel, we have committed no crime, yet we are held here against our wills. You claim to be our liberators, yet you violate every article of war by holding us political prisoners..."

"How dare you scum talk to us about the articles of war!" Major Crimond exploded.

"At ease, Major." I commanded him. He glared at me mutinously. "I'd like to hear what these people have to say. Surely there's no harm in that."

"No sir," he scowled. "However sir, let me point out that his very words indict him. Please note his immediate defense of his slave masters."

"So noted, Major."

Zebrak's countenance seemed to soften. "Thank you, Colonel. Allow me to explain our position. We were orphans, wards of the state. We were raised well at the Institute, we knew nothing of the many atrocities your people say took place there. As to our unusual proclivities, does it matter how we came by them? We are who we are, Colonel, even as you are. It is our fate, each of us, to be what life has made us."

Crimond scoffed at Zebrak's remarks, but I found them troubling. Miss Oleska had yet to speak. I was anxious to hear her voice.

"Young lady, please, do you have anything you wish to tell me."

Those dark eyes met mine, and held them. "I know the secrets of my own soul, Colonel. Can you say the same?"

"I don't understand, what do you mean?"

She had gone mute, staring at my officers and myself with thinly disguised contempt.

"All right, Major, you can have these detainees returned to their quarters now." It was with great difficulty that I broke from her gaze and turned away. We completed the inspection hastily, as the rising heat of the day made the stable area unbearably hot. I thought of Miss Oleska sweltering in that heat, and images of her naked sweating flesh crept into my mind. I shook them off, and continued with my duties, but thoughts of her remained barely suppressed.

That night I could not sleep. My imagination ran wild with scenarios of Staya Oleska bound, shackled, restrained in myriad ways. Shadowy figures moved through my mind, brandishing whips, leather straps, devices only half formed in my waking dream. At the center of it all, the beautiful Staya, her liquid eyes imprecating, "Do you know the secrets of your soul, Colonel?"

I rose from my cot. Buried deep in my foot locker was the parade dress uniform I had not had occasion to wear in many months. I rummaged through the locker and found it. With it was stored the object I sought, my ornamental riding crop. I looked at the crop as if it were the first time I'd seen it. It seemed to possess a presence I had never noted before. I slapped it against my palm, trying to imagine how one could find its sting pleasurable. I struck again, imagining Staya writhing beneath the blow. I was overcome with desire, and for the first time in many years, succumbed to the vice of self-gratification.

All through the following day, as I performed my routine duties, the notion that I should pay a private visit to Staya grew in resolve. My the end of my watch I had reconciled myself to indulging this bizarre, unexpected compulsion. I checked the duty roster, and assured myself that Major Crimond would be elsewhere that evening. Beyond making sure of avoiding the surly intelligence officer, I had formulated no specific plan.

I attired myself in my dress uniform, which I had nonchalantly ordered Captain Nevis to have ironed earlier in the day. I had always thought I looked quite dashing in it. I waited until the camp had settled down for the night, then I tucked the leather crop under my arm, and resolutely made my way to the Special Detainees Quarters.

The same young corporal was on duty. I ordered him to bring Detainee Oleska to the Duty Room. I had rehearsed a dozen unsatisfactory cover stories, but he responded as if my request was the most natural thing in the world. He returned quickly, the woman behind him. As she entered the room he stepped back through the door, shutting it behind him.

"Good evening, Miss Oleska," I began, nervously, "I was thinking about..."

"I'm sure I am aware of what you have been thinking about, my Colonel." Her accent was intoxicating. "I have known a few or so men such as yourself. You are more appealing to me than most."

I stumbled for a reply. She pulled her regulation gray shift over her head.

"Miss Oleska..."

"Staya, I am Staya. And you I call Master."

I felt myself blush. "No, no, Staya, I..."

"You do not desire to use me as you know I enjoy to be used, my Colonel? Is that not why you have come to me tonight, bringing with you your own—what would you say—instrument?"

She pulled the riding crop from beneath my arm. She examined it closely, flexed it, whipped the air with it. As she handed it back to me, she gave a nod of approval.

"It is a very elegant instrument, my Colonel. I would be honored to have a demonstration as to its use."

I stood speechless as she removed her brassiere and panties. She was slender, but not emaciated as were most of her country women in that period. They had taken very good care of her at the Institute.

She crossed the room to me, and pressed her body against me. I looked deeply into her eyes, and succumbed to the desire to kiss her. Her lips were cool and moist and parted ever so slightly against mine. I put my arms around her and pulled her tight against me, kissing her harder. She ran her tongue across my lips and then under my chin, along my jaw line. It sent a shiver of pleasure down my spine. She gently tongued my ear.

"Punish me." she whispered.

I removed her to arms length. Grasping her shoulders, I said "There are other ways to be with a man Staya..."

"You did not come here as a liberator, my Colonel." she replied, with steel in her eyes. "You came to our country to master us. All your talk of freedom masks your dark desires. The Institute made me desire the feel of the whip, my Colonel, but what made you desire to wield it?"

I pushed her away from me. She staggered back against the desk, knocking a stack of papers to the floor.

"Lay across that desk." I told her, a quiver in my voice.

"Is that how you command your troops, my Colonel?" She laughed.

"Get over that desk!" I ordered her with authority. She responded immediately, stretching across the desk and gripping it's far edge. Her toes grazed the floor. The mound of her vagina was visible, embarrassing me. I ran my hand over the cool, smooth flesh of her bottom and felt my desire for her rise. I lined up the crop across the center of her buttocks, pulled it back, and snapped it down. The sound seemed like an explosion to me, but Staya laughed.

"You will have to do much better than that, my Colonel."

I brought it down again, harder, and heard her gasp. The mark of the crop was crimson across her pale flesh, and the sight of it thrilled me. Again I struck her, and again. She began to writhe beneath the blows in a sensuous dance. I covered every portion of her buttocks with blows, the crop singing in my hand. I soon grew confident in its use and playfully painted patterns in red on Staya's undulating bottom. No matter how hard I struck, she seemed to hunger for more, rising off the desk to meet my strokes.The reddest areas of her bottom became tinged with blue. I must have put the crop to her more than one hundred times when I saw the thin line of blood across her buttocks. I dropped my arm to my side, exhausted.

Staya reached between her legs and fondled her vagina. "Take me, Master, please take me."

I dropped the crop, unbuckled my belt and lowered my pants and undershorts. My penis was rigid. I positioned myself behind her, and entered her with one motion. Her tortured flesh was hot against my loins. I thrust into her relentlessly, hard enough to make the desk move. Staya realized a shuddering climax, and almost immediately afterward, I ejaculated inside her.

I stepped back, attempting to regain control of my breath. In an instant Staya was on her knees in front of me, engulfing my member with her mouth. It had begun to soften, but her incessant mouth play quickly reinvigorated it. She picked up the crop from the floor and handed it to me. I did not understand what she wanted me to do. She crossed the room on her knees and sprawled on one of the narrow cots, beckoning me to come to her.

I stood over her and watched as she caressed her own breasts. I began to gently tap them with the crop, and she squirmed with pleasure. I slapped them harder, and her ardor increased.

"Take your hands away," I commanded. She placed one hand behind her head, the other went between her legs. I straddled the cot and alternately cropped her breasts until they grew florid. I moved further up the cot and squeezed my penis between them. Staya ran her tongue around its head and lightly nibbled it. I leaned forward, and plunged deep into her mouth. Without a conscious intent to do so, I was soon ramming myself into her face as arduously as I had into her vagina. She gripped my buttocks and held me to her, even as the force of my thrusts made her gag. In a matter of moments I achieved another orgasm. I felt a stab of shame when I saw my semen on her face, and was shocked to see her wipe it off with her fingers, and then lick them clean.

I fell on to the opposite cot, my head spinning. Staya knelt next to me, her head resting on my chest.

"I've never done anything like that before." I panted.

"I know, my Colonel, but you did very well just the same."

"Thank goodness the Corporal didn't come back in."

"He is used to the routine, my Colonel."

"What do you mean, routine?" I sat up on the cot and took her by the shoulders.

"You did not think you were the first officer in the camp to visit me, did you? Did you not arrange this evening with Major Crimond?"

I raised my hand to slap her, but gained control of myself in time to avoid doing so. To strike her in anger would invalidate everything that had happened between us to a greater extend than the knowledge that she had been with Crimond ever could.

I pulled her to me, and hugged her tightly. She kissed my cheek, then stood and retrieved her clothing. I watched her dress with a profound sadness. I knew I would not come to her again.

When she had dressed she kissed me again and crossed to the door. She started to open it, then turned to me.

"I am what I am, my Colonel, perhaps if I had never been at the Institute I would still be as I am. It does not matter. In my heart I am free to do as I wish, even in your prison."

She shut the door softly behind her. I stared at the place where she had stood, until I realized that the Corporal would soon be returning. I had just gotten my uniform reassembled when he sheepishly scratched at the door. I turned the Duty Room back over to him, and returned to my quarters.

I awoke the next morning with mixed feelings of elation and guilt. I carried this tangle of emotions with me throughout the day, until my mid afternoon briefing with Captain Nevis.

After tediously appraising me of the state of the Camp's daily minutiae, the endless supply requisitions, personnel assignments and detainee complaints, Nevis informed me that he had received a communique from the Intelligence Service on the subject of The Institute for Behavioral Studies. After exhaustive investigation it had been determined that all personnel responsible for criminal acts at the Institute had been killed in the final days of the war.

"So there is no longer any reason to hold the detainees from the Institute, is there?" I asked Nevis.

"None that I know of, Sir." he replied. I dismissed him for the day, and immediately called Crimond. His executive officer answered the telephone, and I was left waiting a full five minutes before Crimond came on the line.

"Yes, sir," he answered at last, "What can I do for you, Colonel Straiton?"

"I've just received word from your people that the investigation into the Institute is closed. I'll send someone over in the morning to take care of integrating those detainees into the general population."

"I'm afraid you can't do that sir."

"What do you mean, I can't do that? There is no longer any reason to hold those people."

"Yes there is sir. They are degenerates, Colonel, perverts of the sickest kind. The Intelligence Service has determined that it would be in the best interest of all involved if we hold all Institute personnel until proper methods of therapy are developed to cure them of their proclivities. Sir."

"That's ridiculous," I sputtered, "I want those detainee..." The line was dead.

I heard Captain Nevis talking in the anteroom. I stuck my head out the door. He was flirting with one of the young women from the secretarial pool. I quietly closed the door, and waited until they had both left. In Nevis' desk drawer I found the file containing blank Detainee Release forms. I quickly filled them out with fictitious names and destinations, and slipped them into my jacket pocket. I then attended evening mess as per my usual routine.

When I finished my meal I crossed the camp to the Special Detainees Quarters. I lingered outside the grounds until I was certain that Crimond and his Officers had departed for the evening, then I entered the compound.

The Corporal snapped to attention as I entered.

"At ease, Corporal. I think you know why I'm here." I winked at him.

"Um, yes sir, you want me to get Detainee Oleska?"

"Yes. And while you're at it, bring Detainee Zebrak and the others too, all the Institute detainees."

His eyes grew wide. Perhaps he tried to envision some bizarre orgy that was just beyond the range of his conception. He swallowed hard, and scampered from the room.

It was a full ten minutes before the Detainees entered, and I was growing concerned that I was too late. At last they arrived, the feisty Zebrak in the lead.

"What do you disturb us now for, Colonel Straiton? Isn't it enough..."

"You're free to go." I interrupted him. "Here are your papers."

He took the release forms and studied them suspiciously.

"But Colonel, I don't understand..."

"You don't have to understand, Zebrak, just go. Walk all night, then get off the main roads. Lose yourselves among the masses."

He handed the forms to the other detainees. I watched him give one to Staya. She looked up and our eyes met.

Zebrak had become giddy with excitement, pumping my hand and slapping my back. I needed all my will power to take my eyes from Staya's.

"Go, Zebrak, lead the others out of here. Now."

He ushered Svor, Polepy and Knin out of the building. He took Staya's arm, but she shook him off. He shrugged and went out.

"You give us this freedom because of last night, my Colonel?"

"No, Staya. I'm doing it because it's the right thing to do. We have no right to judge you."

She kissed me on the cheek, then turned away. "Tonight, you do come as my liberator," she said as she disappeared into the night.

I sat down behind the desk and smoked one of Crimond's cigars. It was nearly dawn before the Corporal got up the nerve to peek into the room. By that time I was sound asleep in my own bunk, and Staya and her fellows were miles from the camp.

When Major Crimond found out what I had done he filed charges against me, and I had to stand before a full court-martial. The more serious charges were mysteriously dropped, perhaps when Crimond realized that I might be able to expose his trysts with Staya, but I was convicted of dereliction of duty, and demoted to the rank of Captain. My subsequent military career has consisted of a procession of unremarkable and meaningless postings. It is my belief that had I not been earlier recognized for my achievement on the battlefield I would have been drummed out of the service. Perhaps that would have been better.

I think of Staya often. All the nights here are hot like that July night was hot, and the local prostitutes are willing to indulge my peculiar tastes. But none of them have those haunting eyes.

I am not bitter. I am not regretful. I have my memories of the war, of great deeds accomplished, of battles won, and honors reaped. I have the knowledge that I did my best for the forsaken masses I was briefly granted the power to help. I have always conducted myself with the honor expected of an agent of the free.

And I know the secrets of my own soul.

Training A Priestess
Andrea J. Horlick

"I love you, my lord," I said, almost whispering. Not the most incongruous thing I might have said, considering he was lying beneath me on the pallet, his cock roused, waiting for me to lower myself. But his eyes were closed, his face immobile. He gave no sign of hearing, or of caring if he had. Then his long-fingered, large-knuckled hands came up and rested on my hips. I felt my usual shudder, half desire, half fear. I obeyed the wordless command.

He always ordered me in silence, just a touch, a glance, a gesture. Sometimes I thought it would have been thus even without his powers. That the connection between us would have been there even were he an ordinary man and I not a seeker of secrets. That my body would have submitted to him even if my soul had not.

He let me do all the work. He might as well have been a marble statue under me, as smooth, as hard, as cold. My head was back, the ends of my unbound hair brushing against his thighs. Sweat trickled down my temples. My lip was between my teeth. The pain and pleasure were about equal.

Then his left hand came off my hip and onto my breast. He seized my nipple between his knuckles and pressed. Hard. Harder. In the instant before my brain said don't make a sound, I let out a low moan. *Take it; the pain will but increase your powers.* I didn't quite know whether he was speaking in my mind or whether I was just remembering past lessons. I bit my lip with more force and tasted the blood.

I opened my eyes again and looked down. The corners of his mouth were turning up just a little. He kept pinching for another minute, then moved his hand back down to my flank and took control. He brought me down harder, faster. He was nearing climax, then. He might be angry with me for not noticing. Keep focused. It was the hardest thing for me to learn.

When he finally opened his eyes, though, I could discern no anger in his expression. None of that cold fury that caused my gut to knot. Not even displeasure, which could be bad enough at times. He studied my face, which was flushed with the sex and slightly wet with tears. A thin trickle of blood ran down from my lower lip and he pulled me closer and licked it away tenderly.

"I was too easy on you tonight by far," he said. "You may count it a blessing when I'm merciful, but only in the short run. If you truly want the power, if you truly wish to learn, my mercy will do you no good."

"Yes, my lord." I closed my eyes again. It was harder for him to read my thoughts when my eyes were closed, when he couldn't look past my pupils into my brain. Harder, but not impossible.

You fear the power. Not what you will have to undergo to obtain it, not the pain of your training. You long for and fear the tests in equal measure, but the power itself terrifies you.

"Yes, my lord," I said again. Lying was both foolish and futile. He rolled us over and pulled out of me, but stayed on top, pinning me to the thin feather mattress, and gently pushed my hair out of my eyes.

"You must make the decision and soon," he said aloud. "Whether you truly want the knowledge. The magik. Or whether all you really want is me."

I shuddered again. Because if all I truly wanted was him, I could never attain my desire. Priests only taught and disciplined initiates. Ordinary women were as nothing to them.

I felt some shame when I joined him in his workroom the next morning. I had given him cause to doubt me, cause to think of me as just some silly woman dabbling in things that were beyond her. But when he looked up from the herbs he was crushing, shaking his long, straight hair back from the beautiful bones of his face, he favored me with a smile. *Don't disparage yourself, Tai. Would a second-degree high priest waste his time on a silly woman?*

He set me to work polishing his silver instruments. It was about all I was good for as yet. Occasionally he would make some comment about what he was doing, either mentally or out loud, but the greater part of my training was just to be next to him, soaking up the power radiating from him. My first month with him, my head and eyes had ached within minutes of being in his presence. But after he was sure of my promise and had taken my virgin's blood, that sickness had eased. Now my awareness of his power was just a quiet humming in my veins. Now I was seriously considering accepting that power for my own. I put down my polishing cloth.

"Only four more weeks," he said. "Four more weeks and I'll pierce your nipples and thread through the chain. Then your only way out will be death, Tai."

"I know, my lord." He was done with his infusion and I heeded his signal to take the vessel from him. I stoppered it carefully with a cork and placed it on the shelf among the other bottles. I knew what that one was for. I only hoped that if I ever saw him use it, it wouldn't be on me.

We'll meditate, then I will test you.

His altar was in the next room, all smooth, sinuous curves of black and white marble. I dropped to my knees as soon as we entered, thinking, not for the first time, how perfectly he melded with the Old Things. He said the chants and I followed, moving my lips but not making a sound. I wasn't yet ready to say the words. I could feel the rush of the power entering him, growing, pulsating. Keep focused. If I kept focused, I should be able to feel my own power increasing, if only incrementally.

The air was thick now, almost visible. I raised my eyes to him, only for a moment. The words of the chant were still coming from him, but his lips were no longer moving. His skin was glowing. Keep focused. I tried to imagine my own skin looking like that, my face in the ecstatic lines of a priest. I tried to find the spark of power inside and make it grow. I trained my sense-memory on the pain-pleasure of the night before, trying to remember when my mind and body had shifted and blended.

Suddenly the thickness of the air rushed out like a vacuum. He was cross-legged in front of me, studying my face once again. "You are ready, Tai?" he said. Or perhaps, "You are ready."

He removed four silver cubes from his pocket and placed them side by side on the altar. *Move them.*

I squeezed shut my eyes. Sense-memory. The glow of power. The cubes were on the inside of my eyelids, weighty in my outstretched hands. Move them. Move them.

With my eyes still tightly closed, I heard rather than saw the first cube go sliding across the smooth marble. My brow was damp with beads of sweat and my hands were beginning to tremble. Then the sweet sound of the second cube following the first. Keep focused. I searched myself for that spark of power as my arms and legs began to shake. Sense-memory. Melting. Glowing. There was nothing left. I fell forward onto my face against the cold stone of the floor.

When I dared to open my eyes, he was still cross-legged in front of me. His face was grave, sorrowful. The two recalcitrant cubes remained on the altar behind his shoulder, mocking me. "I was correct. I was far too easy on you last night. I'm failing in my duty." He placed an image in my mind and the blood rushed from my face.

"Yes, my lord."

It was considered important, nay, crucial, for an initiate to face his or her fears. Even the lower priests, the eighth- and ninth-degree ones, who weren't so facile at reading thoughts and probing minds, had ways of learning just what those deepest fears were. For him it was an effortless thing.

And so I found myself bound on his pallet that night, cold and trembly and cursing my own weakness. I knew my foolishness; he could have made far stronger chains with his mind than these flimsy ropes that tied my wrists. But being restrained, being helpless, had always caused my gorge to rise.

His sharp-boned face was impassive. He played with his silver dagger, looked at my belly. I'd seen men planning to gut a rabbit looking like that. *Use that fear. Turn it into power.* He placed the point of the knife below my left breast and pressed until it just scored my skin. I fought the desire to pull away. There was nowhere for me to go and if I flinched, I might cause him to damage me. He was a second-degree high priest. His control was more than perfect.

He pulled the knife down very, very slowly, down my rib cage, my belly, into my pubic hair. It left just the thinnest cut, a long bleeding scratch that barely stung. My lids were across my eyes, but I could see what he was doing. When I realized it, I felt a surge, a thrill. The first time for that. Focus. He moved the dagger again, lower.

The fear, the vague pain, and the power were all melding and building. Focus. The instant the knife reached my genitals, I looked into his cruel, pleased face without opening my eyes. All at once, I came. The ropes burst from my wrists.

Very good, Tai. Very good. He threw the knife hard into the plaster wall and bent his head to suck the blood off me.

"I love you, my lord," I murmured.

He rewarded me the next few days. I was allowed to hold open his Book, to anoint his body with the proper oils before a sacrifice, to fellate him on the cool stone floor and swallow down his seed, so full of power and life-force it burned all the way down my throat. And perhaps I grew too confident, for on the morning of the fourth day, he called me to the workroom, called me with his mind, and bade me to kneel down, hands behind my back, forehead against the floor.

You will not speak today. You will go about your duties in complete and perfect silence, without a word, without a sound. As the sun begins to set, you will come to my chamber and kneel as you are now. I will ask you one question and you will answer it.

I was not so unwise as to willfully disobey him, but the desire to ask was so overwhelming I had to bite hard into my tongue to keep quiet.

He stepped closer to me and caressed the side of my cheek with his foot. "Of course I'll tell you what the question is to be," he said aloud. I could picture the cold smile on his exquisite face. "You will need time to think of the proper response."

I will ask you how I should discipline you tonight, what your next ordeal is to be. What level of pain and fear is necessary to further expand your mind and soul.

He ordered me then to go and clean his altar room, to scrub the blood from the marble, spread the aromatic herbs, and replenish the candles. My legs were shaking so much I could barely rise from my cramped position.

I was at the doorway when he stopped me. "I know I can trust you, Tai," he said, "not to be too easy on yourself."

I spent the rest of the day in a haze of apprehension and anticipation. At noon hour I sat in the common room at a table with the other initiates, unable—and unwilling at any rate—to participate in the conversation. I sipped the coolish water from my wooden cup but left my bowl untouched. My belly rebelled at the very thought of food.

Then suddenly he was behind me. I felt the rush of power from him before he was even close enough to touch me.

There's a time for fasting, Tai, and a time when one must eat to keep up one's strength. He held a thick chunk of bread soaked in wild honey to my lips and fed it to me, a bite at a time. When it was gone, he had me suck all traces of the stickiness from his fingers.

"Come. I have more work for you." I felt the awed and envious glances of the other initiates on my back as he led me out.

A couple of hours before dusk, he set me a few more simple tasks and left me alone. He was doing me a great honor, I knew, allowing me to offer up my agony freely. As I polished a few of his instruments and swept out the room, I thought about what I would say when he asked the question. Not that I was unsure of what my answer would be. I just wanted to give it elegantly, no hesitations, no trembling in my voice. I wanted, more than anything, to make him proud of me.

* * *

He was cross-legged on his pallet when I entered, no longer meditating, but with the glow on his skin and the thickness in the air that meant he had been. I assumed my position and waited. It was some minutes before he decided to take notice of me.

"What shall I do to you, then? Speak now, Tai." *You may look at me as you answer.*

I pulled myself into a full kneeling position and raised my eyes to the region of his mouth. He pressed his lips together and reached out to push my chin up another inch until our eyes locked. "My lord," I said, fighting to keep my voice pitched low and steady. "You have never beaten me. Please, tonight, whip me. Help me conquer that pain."

His lips twitched into half a smile and he removed something from beneath the pallet. A switch. The perfect switch, two and a half feet long, thin and flexible and strong. I wondered if he had gone out of the temple grounds and into the forest that afternoon to cut it, or whether he had just conjured it. And just the one switch, no extras in case it snapped as he flogged me. It was as if he knew he could whip me with it all night and it would never break.

He tucked it under his arm and came off the mattress to help me to my feet. With great gentleness he unfastened my robe and pushed it off my shoulders. He bent me across the pallet, my buttocks and thighs at just the angle he wanted.

No bonds this time. Answering my thought. *You will keep yourself still. Flow into the pain, Tai. Accept it.*

"Yes, my lord."

No. No more talking.

He took one more thing from beneath the pallet. A gag. He placed it into my mouth and fastened it carefully underneath my hair. "A little mercy for you. Now you need concentrate only on not moving, not on your silence."

I waited for him to begin, my eyes closed against the rough blanket, sweat forming already on my naked body in the coolness of the room, every sense heightened with dread and longing. I could almost hear it as he stepped back from me and flexed the switch between his hands.

Then he started. Lightly at first, mild, stinging blows that landed right where my buttocks and thighs joined. But soon the strokes increased in intensity, cutting into my tender skin, raising hot welts wherever the switch touched. I tried to count the strokes in an attempt to master the pain, but as the number approached a hundred, the pain was mastering me.

I bit against my gag and the blanket beneath my cheek grew damp. Finally, I began to flinch ever so slightly at each blow. He reached out with his mind and steadied me.

Don't struggle. Focus. He held my mind with his, even as he continued to whip me, and I felt his power merging with the beginnings of my own. I found that place in me that was beyond pain. The burning of my lacerated skin melded into sweet pleasure, and as he pulled out of my mind, the pleasure remained.

As I realized it, as I realized that I was in control of my body, my spirit, my own power, I started to come, not with my genitals alone, but with my whole self. As I began to slip from consciousness, he spoke in my mind once more. *Just a taste, Tai, just a taste of what will be yours.*

I woke just before dawn in his arms on the narrow bed. Our hair was tangled together, wrapped around our bodies like a sheet, and one of his big hands cupped my buttock. I had never seen him asleep. I looked at his face,

its harsh beauty softened now, and wished I dared to
reach out and stroke his cheek. Instead I closed my eyes
again, concentrated on his warm breath in my face and
the smoothness of his skin against mine, hoping he
would want the use of me when he woke. I was
beginning to drift back into contented sleep when the
thought struck me. The flesh beneath his hand should
still be raw, tender. But it was not.

I reached my own hand back, feeling for the welts
and stripes that had been there only hours before. They
were gone, my skin whole and unmarked and no longer
sore.

"Oh, my lord," I whispered. Tears welled up and
spilled onto my cheeks. I cried quietly so as not to rouse
him.

The next time he had me move the cubes, I did it with
very little trouble. His approval covered me like a warm
blanket and I felt my face flush worse than it did from
sex. *You needed to trust yourself, Tai. You needed to give up all
control and then take it back. You're almost ready for the final
test now. Pass that and I'll pierce you and make you ours.*

"And you know now that you do want it." It was
even rarer now that he bothered to speak to me in words.
In the last week I'd almost forgotten what his voice
sounded like.

"I do want it, my lord." I reached up and brushed a
piece of hair from my eyes. He'd already shaved the left
side of my head, like a priestess, but I couldn't braid the
other side till I proved myself in the final test. I went
unclothed all the time now too, like a priestess, and I'd
begun to forget the feeling of cloth against my flesh as
well.

Tomorrow then. And your piercing two days after that.
He was eager for it, more so even than I. It was likewise

his final test. If I were successful, he would be a first-degree high priest, unbelievably powerful, a god walking among men.

And as much as we both wanted it, we knew the price. Any fool, any child, could tell you power had a price. I reached my hand out and trailed it longingly down his chest, but he caught my wrist, his expression stern. *No. Go now and meditate through the night.*

"Yes, my lord."

He had alerted the two eldest priests and they came at dawn to get me from my vigil. My knees were stiff from kneeling, my body woozy and my head buzzing from lack of sleep. But the power was singing through my blood. I could do it. I would do it.

They led me by my arms to his altar room. His body was sleek and shining against the black and white marble, his hair cascading backwards to the floor. His silver dagger was between his teeth. He crossed his arms over his chest, a sacrificial posture.

I salute you, my lord, and thank you for my training, I tried in my head and was gratified to see they could all hear me without effort. I bent my head to his and took the knife with my own mouth. The two elders began the chant, low and strong. The air grew syrupy. His face was that of a corpse and his breaths so shallow, his chest barely rose and fell. I transferred the knife from my mouth to my left hand and gathered all the power in the room to myself, chanting out loud for the very first time. The Old Words were like sugared poison on my tongue.

I stepped around to the foot of the altar and paused. His cock was roused, massively erect against the tight muscle of his abdomen. I took it in my right hand. All the old forces, life, death, and procreation, sang in me. I held the silver knife against the root of his penis. The old men chanted louder. There was no flicker of movement from him. The air was impossibly opaque.

Know that I loved you too, Tai.

I sliced through in one quick stroke as the chanting rose to a scream. Blood gushed warm over my hands. The even greater rush of power dazzled me and I drew it in, further in, and willed the bleeding to stop. I watched the skin begin to draw together on the wound. Keep focused. Joy bubbled up as I watched myself healing him, making him whole, yet not whole, yet more than what he was.

My lord. I said it one last time as my knees collapsed and my body slumped onto the cold stone floor. *My lord.*

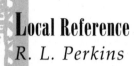

Local Reference
R. L. Perkins

She tugged at the cuffs buckled around her wrists, cursing again her large hands and narrow wrists. The wide leather cuffs were padlocked to a chain that was bolted securely to the bed frame. There was simply no way for her to escape. She looked over her shoulder at the figure standing above her prone body, the one she knew only as `Sir'. His face was classically handsome, the lines and planes of his chiseled features picked out in soft contrast by the glow from the 3D television set. His body was strongly muscled without that over-developed look that too many men she knew thought attractive to women. His lips were fuller than most men's and curved in a perpetual smile. His eyes were piercing blue and seemed to sense her most intimate secrets. She had encountered him a few short weeks ago, at the shuttle port, or maybe it was at the controversial android ballet opening. Funny that she couldn't remember. At times like this she was never really sure of anything.

Sir wrapped the fingers of his hand in her silken blonde hair and pulled her head back. He kissed her, his tongue pushing easily past her lips to explore her mouth. The kiss was slow, arrogantly casual, as if he had all night to torment her and felt no pressure to rush things. He broke the kiss and released her hair. She felt a tickle as nano machines programmed with the latest in hair styles labored to restore her original coif.

His hand drifted down the curves of her back, following the ridge of her spine until it disappeared above the cleft of her buttocks. He began stroking her bottom with an upsweeping motion. She buried her face between her outstretched arms and lifted her hips off the bed to meet his hand. The slap was as sharp as it was sudden, the sound echoing in her ears. The outline of his hand burned like a brand on her buttock.

She strained to lift her hips higher for him. He slapped her again before resuming his caresses. She hated this position, knowing it left her completely exposed. She fancied men found her body attractive. The best trainer that her money could buy saw to it that she was as firm and toned as a TV starlet. Her wardrobe was full of plunging backs, daring decolletage, and skirts slit to her hip; carefully tailored to show off her body. With a practiced walk she could reward her gawking male admirers with a precisely controlled glimpse of sculpted leg. She loved those moments, watching the men around her responding like children teased with a bit of chocolate too rich for their tongues. But now Sir's strong hands were spreading her open, reducing her to a common whore. She knew she was already wet, that he could sense it and would know that he had done that to her. That he stripped her not only of clothing, but of dignity as well.

He tasted her, his lips soft and warm against her cunt. He stroked her clit with his tongue, cruelly teasing her, bringing her to the ragged edge of orgasm only to hold her trapped in elegant torture. His sense of her arousal was uncanny; he could maintain her balanced on the point of orgasmic release with merciless precision. Their first time together he had reduced her to tearful begging. Afterwards she had thrown him out, sworn never to see him again. Their second time she had screamed in her frustration until he paused long enough to gag her. When she had tried to fight him, he had tied her legs spread straining wide. She had even once tried to out maneuver him by forcing herself to lie limp and unresponsive. Her body had given her away, providing him with a steady flow of her juices in response to his tireless mouth.

She moaned pitifully into the satin-cased pillow. Her need had swollen from tingling passion to a painful pressure spreading through her belly, cramping the muscles of her back and shoulders. Her cunt twitched and spasmed, grasping at emptiness with each stroke of his tongue. She hated his mouth. She obsessed over his mouth. She wanted to live in his mouth.

When he finally took his mouth away she realized that she had been begging again. He took her in his arms and rolled her limp, frustrated body onto her back. His tongue flicked over her nipples like a candle flame. She barely bit back a scream when he trapped her right nipple between his teeth. She could smell her sex on his lips. He stood and took her ankles in his hand, lifting her legs straight up in the air and shifting her hips to the edge of the bed. His fingers stroked her face, lightly tracing the line of cheekbone below soft skin. She turned her head to catch his thumb with her mouth. He stepped back, his thumb making a wet popping sound as he pulled it from her mouth. He untied his robe and let it fall to the floor. He was already erect and sheathed in latex. Sir was better endowed than any man she had been with, the biggest she had ever seen. She had been intimidated at first, now she was enraptured. He stroked himself in front of her face. She reached for him with her mouth, letting her legs droop.

He caught the soles of her bare feet in his hand and tsked at her. He lifted her by her ankles, raising her hips completely off the bed. The spanking wasn't as hard as she had expected. She was surprised when it didn't stop after a couple of slaps. Her blood pooled in her head and the sound of her pulse began to beat in time with Sir's hand on her bottom. Each stroke was harder than its predecessor until it took all her concentration not to cry out with each stroke. Her buttocks felt on fire, and she hoped he had hurt his god damn hand.

He lowered her onto the bed and hugged her legs to his chest. The head of his cock spread the swollen lips of her cunt. His hips slowly pressed forward and back, each time sliding infinitesimally deeper into her before withdrawing. She bit at the inside of her own arm trying in vain to focus herself against the new assault. He kept his slow infuriating rhythm until his cock finally filled her. Her torment continued, as deep as he was going into her, he was just too slow to push her over her orgasmic edge. Her cunt clenched trying to grasp his cock, her hips bucked trying to steal that vital sensation he withheld. He grabbed her hips, pinning her against the mattress.

"Sir," she said, "Sir, please."

He smiled down at her, his face impassive, his hips keeping slow, perfect time.

"Sir, I can't take it anymore. Please, Sir. Please."

Slowly filling her, then easing away.

"Please."

Stretching her vagina...

"Sir, please..."

Then hollow and empty.

"God damn it! Stop teasing and fuck me, will you! I want it now!"

He stopped mid-stroke. He tsked again and withdrew his cock. He paused to steady her legs in the air before turning away.

It took every bit of her remaining strength to hold her legs up without his support. Her toes traced lazy arcs in the air before she found the strength to steady herself. Sir went to the armoire where she stored her toys. He turned to face her and displayed an enormous rubber phallus.

The thing was the size of her arm. She envisioned of dying on such a cock, impaled through her vagina by a gigantic penis, orgasming with her last breath as it filled her body. She shivered with excitement. Sir saw it and immediately responded.

He pushed the head of it between the lips of her cunt and rested its base on the base of his own organ. He spread her legs in a `V' and began to push the giant dildo into her. Her lungs felt paralyzed as it slid into her, stretching her to her absolute limit. It was halfway inside her when she felt the head of his cock press insistently against her anus. He centered it with his hand. Fear shot through her, she tensed to block his passage. He leaned over her and the head of his cock painfully entered her. She pulled on her cuffs and chain futilely trying to yank herself off him. He held her legs tight in his arms as he continued to push deeper. The dildo filled her; still he didn't stop until his cock was buried half way into her ass. She had never felt so full. She tried to speak, to beg him to stop, but couldn't shape the words. He smiled that infuriating quiescent smile of his and covered her mouth with his hand. He eased his hips back minutely, and she forced herself to relax. A heartbeat later he drove himself into her.

She began screaming, not sure if her screams were from pain or the intensity of the orgasms that exploded through her body. She bit at Sir's hand and tasted salty wetness. He refused to let go as she continued to scream. He fucked her hard and fast, pumping both himself and the dildo into her. Her orgasms continued until she couldn't breath, silencing her screams. He continued steadily hammering into her until she slipped into a faint.

When she came to, gasping for air, she saw he still stood beside her bed, peeling away the spent condom. The head of his uncovered cock glistened. She wanted to taste it, but was too weak to fight her way to him. She watched him working his cock and balls with a peculiar squeezing stroke. She thought she could feel the heat of his balls warming the her skin. He aimed his cock into the air like an artillery piece and fired. The thick while stream of his cum arced over her belly and splashed onto her heaving breasts. The droplets burned her like molten wax and trailed bright stripes of pain as they ran down her skin.

He stroked her breasts and belly with his finger tips as she caught her breath and lay basking in her own private afterglow. His hands traced fractal whorls with mathematical precision in the sweat coating her skin, his fingers provided the perfect amount of pressure to relax her. After a few minutes she began to stir.

"Fragile," she whispered.

The padlock opened with a soft click as Sir stepped back. His face was utterly blank.

"Sir, store!"

Sir pivoted and returned to the armoire that dominated the corner of the small bedroom.

The woman pushed the chain under the coarse mattress before painfully struggling to her feet. Standing for hours without moving in front of Loom 27B at the Algonquin Textile Mill Number Six irritated the arthritis that stiffened joints in her short legs. She wanted to quit, the dole would pay for her dingy rooms. But without the steady paycheck the credit company would back up a truck to her door and haul the android and her 3D HighDef television set away. She limped to the cabinet and detached the dildo from its adapter, and with a counterclockwise twist removed Sir's standard penis. She made her way to the bathroom fighting her embarrassing tendency to waddle. She washed the appliances in the sink with soap and water, then dried them on a dingy hand towel. She tied her coarse hair back before splashing cool water on her face. She was picking the remaining hardened droplets of paraffin from her flaccid breasts when she heard the theme music from her favorite program, the one with that skinny blonde bitch, erupt from the TV speaker on her battered bureau.

She put the penises away in their storage drawer, pausing to run her fingers over the other variations that Sir could be equipped with. She lifted the long and flexible black penis and fondled it. That would be for tomorrow, she though to herself. She sprayed Sir's bitten hand with a repair solution. Nano machines suspended in the fluid would repair the torn synthetic skin overnight. She kissed him on his cooling lips.

"I love you, Sir," she said to the android as she closed its cabinet and reached for the TV remote. Maybe this time that little blonde cock tease would get what was fucking coming to her.

Cyber Knight
Gary Bowen

I walked into the room and noticed the usual collection of wannabe mistresses in push up bras and self-proclaimed doms in black leather pants; I scanned past them quickly, looking, looking... I was new here, or at least, this incarnation of me was, it remained to be seen how effective an interface I had designed. I'd spent a lot of time working out the details: tall, lithe, androgynous, with a gravity defying white blond mohawk, two gold earrings, white spandex tights, combat boots, and a lot of red body paint zigzagging across my arms and making mystical signs on my chest and back. A pseudo-dom detached himself from the crowd, gliding over to me.

"Top or bottom?" were his first words to me.

"None of your business," I replied, not liking his attitude.

He drew himself up to his full height, an imposing six four here in Cyberland. I did the mental arithmetic and figured in the real world he must be five nine, max. Overcompensation, you know.

"That's Sir Adam to you," he pronounced.

It was times like this I really missed my nicotine addiction. Chording furiously in the real world, I programmed a cigarette to appear in my simulcrum's hand, complete with ivory holder a la Hollywood. I blew smoke at him. "Not until you've earned it."

His eyes darkened. "That can be arranged."

"I doubt it." I turned my back on him and walked into the next room.

"I didn't give you permission to leave!" he snarled at my back. I kept walking. It was Cyberland, nobody could touch me. I was safely back at my console, chording the programs necessary to sustain an elaborate—and boring—game of make believe.

The next room wasn't as well developed at the room I'd left; it was a simple box with two doors, and a not very good simulcrum of a bar. A couple of girls with purple hair and pierced noses were standing together.

"What a dive," I said out loud. Six months ago I'd thought it was Happily Ever After Land. Yeah, me and my console were going places. We were gonna be a bigshot virtual reality team. Wrong. Cyberland was populated by as many losers as the real world. And now I was in a really pissy mood, prepared to act the role of the Bottom from Hell because I was bored.

I approached the bar, leaned my elbow on it, and yelled, "What does it take to get some beer around here?"

The bartender materialized. "A little courtesy," he replied mildly. He was bald on top, wearing a white dress shirt with black garters on his sleeves, and a black leather vest. I couldn't recall ever meeting a bald man in cyberspace before, aside from the Neo Goths who shaved their heads on purpose. When you can be anything you wanna be, nobody chooses to be bald. I glanced over the bar. Not only bald, but rotund. Not seriously rotund, not by real world standards, but compared to the standard issue svelte bodies of Cyberland, he was a definite anomaly.

"You're new," I said.

"No, I'm old. Just been playing other roles for a while."

His simulcrum was perfect, right down to the worn crotch of his blue jeans and the ripped knees. His work boots were scuffed even. He looked really real.

"Can I get a beer, please?" I asked, wondering if he was a top or a bottom. I wasn't so crass as the pseudo-dom who gotten in my face, but all the same, I wanted to know.

He poured beer, the illusion perfect. He was good. Either he'd done this a million times before, or he could program as fast as I could. I decided to test his ingenuity. I waved my cigarette holder at him. "Light?"

He flicked a yellow plastic Bic at me. Good. Still, lighters were small objects, he might actually be able to chord that fast. I racked my brain for another test. "Peanuts?"

A package appeared, and by ghod if it didn't look like the Planters I got in the real world. No hesitation, he just reached under the bar and there it was. I grabbed the package and ripped it open. Peanuts, each one slightly different, spilled out. That was a heck of a lot of programming. But he might be equipped with an array of pre-made micro programs to enhance the game of playing bartender. Some people got that obsessive about their cyber roles. Yet, the bar itself was crude.

I patted the counter top. "Not your work, I take it."

"No, not mine."

I nodded. It's considered rude for more skilled programmers to alter objects made by others. You can add anything you like to a room, but you can't change what's already there. Such is the unspoken code of Cyberland. My fingers chorded like lightning, and now my cigarette was animated, burning and creating ash as if it were a real cigarette. "Ashtray?"

He put one on the bar, a plain round glass one. Easy, but in keeping with his low key approach to everything. "Dart board?"

He turned around, produced a dart board, darts
stuck in the target, quivering as he let it thump onto the
bar. Wow.

"Chess?"

He produced a box, unfolded the board, and set up
the individual pieces. "You play?" he asked casually, as if
organizing thirty-two pieces of pseudo-plastic was no
work at all.

"A little," I replied.

"I'll play you," he said.

"Okay. What're the stakes?"

"I win, I get to whip your smart ass."

My blood quickened. "And if you lose?"

His face was bland, but the laugh lines around his
eyes crinkled. "What do you want from me?"

"A good game," I responded promptly. What did I
want? To be entertained. To be topped by somebody who
knew how to do it right, who could take whatever was at
hand—riding crop, cigarette, chess board—and use it to
dominate me, no matter how I struggled. That was the
fundamental challenge of sensuous magic; the dom had
to know how to weave a spell that paralyzed his sub and
made him submit. Because in truth, there was nothing an
ethical dom could do to force a rebellious sub into
compliance. It was all a mind game.

"I see. You'll play for pride. You win, you get to feel
superior and continue playing the arrogant asshole. You
lose..." he shrugged.

His words irked me, but they touched something too.
"Whatever. Suppose I think about it while we play, and
when I decide I let you know?"

He smiled faintly. "All right." He picked up a black
and white pawn, held them in two beefy hands. I pointed,
he opened his hand to reveal the white pawn.

I moved first. I wasn't good at chess, I knew it. In
that he had mistaken me. He was going to win. No doubt

about it. Unless he was awful, but I doubted that. My heart throbbed in my chest, and I felt heat coursing through my veins. This was stupid. Why didn't I just say, "Whip me, beat me, make me write bad checks?" The two of us could go off to play without this display of mental machismo.

He moved in response, and I moved quickly, not knowing what would happen to the pieces. He countered with deliberate calm. I lost a pawn. No biggie. He watched me over the pieces, and I stared at the board. What would he do to me? I was slow to move my piece, too preoccupied with the inevitable end to pay much attention to how I rapidly I was losing. He contemplated the board for long moments, and I waited, fingers poised to chord my response. We each made several more moves. "Check," he said.

"You win." I disappeared.

I set down the chording balls and removed the helmet from my head. I was sweating, and I was half hard. I ran my fingers through my own short cropped brown hair. Then I took the mohawked interface and moved it to storage. It wasn't right. Something had almost happened in there. I brooded at my console, then donned the helmet and picked up my chording balls again. I entered my own space, the one that was mine all mine, that nobody could get to unless I let them. The foyer was a plain dark room, a little misty. A single spot light shown down from above, but there was no lamp casting it. I stood in the middle and thought. I didn't feel like going to any of the places I'd made, and I didn't feel like going to anybody else's place either. I decided the foyer was as good a place as any to do my programming for a new interface.

What now? The opposite of the mohawk, I didn't want to be recognized. Okay, short and dark haired, with a buzzcut. Square jaw, broken nose. Bull neck, squat, powerful chest. Long arms. Long legs. Black leather pants. And taking a cue from the perfectly imperfect bartender, signs of wear along the seams and crotch, and serious scuffs on the knees. Steel toed boots, also scuffed. A black tee shirt with the Cyberland logo on it. I spent a lot of time adding in the little details: tattoos and earrings, debating the exact pattern of the studded leather belt. But I had no sense of the man I was creating. He looked good, but he was just an interface. I shoved him into storage.

What could I do? Who could I be that would be enough me to be a real person, but was enough not-me to be safe? I decided to copy and edit the mohawk. I kept the hair, added an earring. I switched to black leather pants and a black leather vest, remembering to add the wear marks. I decided on a button fly and no belt. Better. But he'd still recognize me if I ran into him again. Having chickened out, I didn't particularly want to meet him. I colored the mohawk purple. Forget it, not me. I changed it back to Billy Idol blond. I'd just have to stay out of the club rooms for a while. He'd forget in a couple of days.

I dropped back into Cyberland, choosing to arrive on the veranda. White wicker chairs were placed all along an old fashioned Victorian porch, white, complete with elaborate gingerbread. Examining the fretwork with a programmer's eye, I saw it was one intricate pattern endlessly repeated. Computers are great at duplication. I looked across the wildflower meadow to the distant mountains: texture mapped. But it looked pretty. The only other people were a couple of girls in white corsets and pantaloons servicing a proper British gentleman at the far end; I ignored them. I settled in a chair, slung one knee over the arm, and started chording. Clouds were not easy, I had to reference a couple of texts before I managed something halfway reasonable. I kept fiddling with them, and finally got a pretty decent bit of cumulus to drift over the mountains. I was at work programming their shadows to follow them across the mountains when another man joined me on the veranda. He was tall and barrel chested, with a black tee shirt and leather pants. His black hair was cut short and he wore mirrored sunglasses. He settled a few chairs down from me, and I ignored him. I was conducting some experiments back in my own space, and bit by bit ported the results up to Cyberland. Clouds crowded the sky, and lightning flashed distantly. Thunder growled. I relaxed, letting my storm simulation play itself out in the distance.

Creation always left me feeling pleasantly tired, and a little horny. This being Cyberland, I started fondling my crotch. No reason why I shouldn't do what I felt like doing—that was why Cyberland existed. To play out unspeakable fantasies without paying the consequences. I unbuttoned my fly and took it out. Just to amuse myself I made my dick long and pointy, with its foreskin still attached, topped off by a gold Prince Albert. Having a Prince Albert means never losing your keys.

I chorded a bit more, and a cool breeze smelling of rain washed over the veranda from the mountain. The girls didn't notice, but the cool breeze caressing my balls felt good to me. The mirrored sunglasses of the single man turned my way, and I watched myself reflected in them, pulling on my cock with long hard strokes. Then he rose, and maneuvering around the abundant wicker furniture, placed a small black knight on the table before me. He walked on, turning the corner of the veranda while I stared at the object he had left.

It was a piece from the chess piece we had used earlier in the evening. I stuffed my dick back in my pants and jumped up, buttoning as I tripped over the furniture and tried to follow him. But he was gone, and the only person on the veranda was a mistress in latex miniskirt and black bustier, riding crop in her hand, smoking. Damn.

I examined the chess piece. It was an elegant piece of programming, and I hunted for the programmer's mark. JDBlack. Nothing more. No title or nickname, no symbol or logo, nothing. Just the name. I hit the reference tools and called up info on JDBlack.

"I'm sorry," the computer murmured in my ear. "That is a restricted account. No information is available."

Damn. I teleported back to the bar.

Half a dozen poseurs in various shades of black were occupying the room, a few of them hoisting beer mugs. I recognized JDBlack's work: the mugs were perfect imitations of the real world. He had been here, and not long ago. How long had he sat on the veranda while I made clouds? A long time. Suspicion seized me, I accessed my own data.

"Account queried at 02:30:45 by Unknown User." It had been easy for him to find me. I had simply modified the old simulcrum instead of cloning it—cloning would have identified it as a new object and provided it with a new number. I cloned myself, got a new ID number, and junked the old simulcrum. Now I was brand new and he couldn't track me by my ID number. When I walked away I ghosted, and now there were two of me in the room. No program is perfect, I'd confused it by cloning myself in active space. I chorded some more, and at last my ghost disappeared. A beer appeared at my elbow.

"Genuine Miller Draft," he said.

I looked over the counter at him, noticed the bald spot was shiny. I backed away. I didn't want him to think I'd been looking for him, yet I couldn't think of any plausible prevarication. I disappeared again.

I jumped back to the veranda, that being the most recent place and therefore instantly accessible off of my automated menu. But if he were following me, that would be the first place he'd guess. I thought fast, and chorded the ID for the Well of Lost Souls.

The Well was made of damp granite blocks, with sunlight shining down, and niches carved into the sides at intervals. It was about twenty-six feet across, experimentation having proved that was the greatest distance at which you could easily talk to someone perched across from you. Psychologically easy—feet or miles didn't matter in Cyberland, but as your simulcrum looked across the space, you reacted as if it was real. The Goths had discovered the Well of Lost Souls and loved it, but they weren't here tonight. Georgie was on his usual perch, rocking back and forth, singing to himself in strange detached sentences, red hair spiked all over his head. I liked Georgie. He was a reality unto himself. His signature was on many of the additions to the Well of Lost Souls, and all of them were grotesque, small, and subtle. He was especially fond of creating tortured rock faces that would howl or whimper if you bumped into them.

"You're being followed," he said, startling me.

"Damn!" I looked around, but nobody was near us.

"Invisible," he added.

That chilled me. Only operators had the privilege of being invisible. They stalked Cyberland, administering a rude and almost undetectable kind of justice. If I felt wronged, I could ask for an operator to intervene. I'd never see them and neither would anybody else. Either the problem would be solved, or it would not. Nobody ever knew for sure. If an obnoxious jerk suddenly disappeared, was it because he got bored and left? Or was it because an operator had kicked him off? I didn't know. I remembered my sullenness earlier in the evening,

and was glad JDBlack had cut me a break. Some
operators are real hard cases.

"Hey Chess!" I yelled while scanning the references
for info on operators. Another dead end. Nobody
answered my hail, but Georgie started crawling up the
wall like a fly.

"You leaving me, Georgie?"

"I may be crazy, but I'm not stupid," he replied, and
squeezed himself so thin he could slide down a
gargoyle's throat. He liked disturbing entrances and exits
of that sort. Now I was alone, except for his gargoyles. I
scanned each of them, but I had seen them all before.
Nothing new, nothing that could be an operator in
disguise. But then, he was invisible, he had no need of
disguise. Water began to run down the wall, and dripped
onto my ledge. It pooled in a shallow depression, then
poured over the edge. I glanced down at the wetness, and
it was red.

"Georgie!" I yelled. That was just like Georgie. He
loved gruesome effects. If Georgie wasn't spaced out in
Cyberland, he'd have been conducting experiments on
unwilling subjects in the real world. I wished he hadn't
left. I messaged him.

"Not my program," was his reply.

Mist began to drift down from above, occluding the
sunlight that graced the chamber. It swelled in lazy,
swirling spirals, growing larger and denser, becoming a
form, arms and head shaping themselves above an
indeterminate blotch. A pebble fell, bouncing from ledge
to ledge, then dropping straight down towards the
bottom. "You'll never hear it splash," a woman's voice
said.

I pressed myself back against the wall. The mist
continued to accumulate, gradually becoming a woman
in a long dress, pale grey in color, form fuzzy around the
edges, merging with the mist in the well.

"JDBlack?" I asked. I had assumed JD was male because that was the form I first saw. But there was no reason why a person should not appear as either gender. Most people, like me, stuck with their biological gender, but again, that was a psychological limit, not a real one. Limits had to be artificially created in Cyberland. I had programmed the Well of Lost Souls to have gravity, if you fell off your ledge, you fell. It was the only place in Cyberland that actually had gravity. Anywhere else, if you set a beer mug floating in the air, it stayed.

The form did not fall, and seeing it defy my rules did not reassure me. "Why are you following me?"

"I thought you might like women better."

"I don't." I programmed rapidly, and cloned it a couple dozen times. Now I had a stack of softball sized rocks beneath my hand. I picked one up and threw it. It passed right through the ghost with no effect.

"Why are you afraid of me?"

"Because I don't know what you are!" My voiced echoed loudly, another detail of my programming. It spooked me, and I hated myself for being such a good programmer. She/he/it was taking advantage of what I had made to freak me out. I teleported.

I landed in the middle of the wildflower meadow, yellow and pink and white flowers growing right through me. The meadow had been programmed for image only, it didn't act like a real meadow. The remnants of my storm were clearing away overhead. I felt safe with daisies sprouting through my stomach while my storm drifted overhead. The meadow was a peaceful place. I relaxed, checked my program, gave it a couple of adjustments, and set it to storm at random intervals. I also scheduled a storm for every Tuesday night at eight pm. Then I headed back to the veranda.

And he was there, standing at the top of the steps, male, brush cut, black clothes, thoroughly real. I stared into his mirrored shades for a long moment, but before I could make up my mind what to do he turned and walked away. He took a seat in a chair, which creaked under him. Details! The chairs had never creaked before. He was a hell of a programmer. He propped one foot on the coffee table, and three glossy magazines appeared on the table top, along with a pot of orange Gerbera daisies. A Tiffany lamp appeared on the end table, and he switched it on. It got suddenly dark, and I looked up to see the sun setting behind the Mansion in a burst of orange light, fading away in a matter of minutes.

"You're an wizard," I said.

He nodded. Nobody else could fiddle with basic operations like the progression of time in Cyberland. Usually internal time ran at approximately twice real world speed. But he wanted it to be night, and lo, it was night.

Night. I took the chess piece from my pocket. Knight. It makes the oblique moves. It threatens, but its path is forked and hard to follow. It surprises.

He watched me.

I turned the piece in my hands, wondering, feeling a tension in my lower belly as my cock began to point towards him. I walked nonchalantly up from the wildflowers, colored petals clinging to my leather jeans as if by static electricity. I crossed the narrow strip of lawn and mounted the stairs. I sat on the railing opposite him. Not to be outdone, I created a pot of sweetly scented red geraniums, and duplicated it, hanging pots in every other arch of the gingerbread. It was a very long porch, I made six pots.

His lip curled, and it might have been a smile, but I wasn't sure. "You like this place."

"Yes."

He nodded. "I do too. Godfrey made it."

I'd heard about Godfrey 'God' Sullivan. He reputedly owned the machine that housed Cyberland. He had built the first virtual rooms, designed the protocols that governed it, simplified the coding so that anybody with half a brain could learn to program it if they wanted to. "Did you know him?"

"Yes."

"You're one of the Twelve."

He shrugged.

I wanted to ask him what he wanted with me, but I was afraid. Direct questions of that sort are rude. I accessed the menus, and there, in the 'About this Application' section, was a listing of the thirteen talents who had made Cyberland. Godfrey 'God' Sullivan was listed as Creator, and below him were his twelve disciples, 'JDBlack' included.

"Wow."

"Does it matter?"

Of course it mattered! I was flattered to have one of the greatest wizards of all time paying attention to me. But I remembered my unease in the Well of Lost Souls. "You're playing with me."

He laughed long and hard, the mirrored glasses almost falling off. "I'm trying. But you keep running away."

I ground my teeth in chagrin and decided I didn't have to listen to that. I popped into the White Queen's dungeon.

She was working over a pair of twins, boys. I checked their signatures, both were made by the same man. Yeah, every kink, twins, too. No pun intended. I slipped along the back, working my way behind the people standing and watching her flog the hapless simulcrums.

Personally, I don't see much point to virtual
sadomasochism, you can't feel anything unless you've
got a great program or a vivid imagination. I mingled
with the crowd at the back of the room and admired the
set. The White Queen put on a great show: the room was
a medieval torture chamber straight out of Hollywood.
Torches in sconces burned steadily, casting light
throughout the room. The White Queen was dressed in a
white fur bikini with ornamental chain mail and a crown
on her head. Her armor jingled as she moved, her tits
jiggled, and her hips swayed. Watching her was like
watching jello do the shimmy.

JDBlack didn't appear. I was disappointed, I had
really expected him to follow me. I had counted on it
even.

I watched the White Queen pause to stroke her
delirious victims, then materializing a toy out of thin air,
she slipped a large size dildo into the ass of the twin on
the left. He groaned and writhed, and she reached around
front and pinched his tits. He was a pretty boy, shoulder
length black hair, and completely nude body, with only a
little bit of dark fur in his crotch and up the crack of his
ass. She unchained the other twin, and jerking him to his
knees, set him in front of the standing twin, and made
him give himself head.

The conceit amused me, and I cloned myself. Now I
was looking at myself, and my other self was looking at
me. With a laugh we started kissing. It was boring
though: no suspense. We each knew what was going to
happen next. I deleted one of my selves. Where was
JDBlack?

I wandered out of the torture chamber, passed various
leather folk including a fairy in a lavender tutu with
codpiece, and found myself at last on the balcony

overlooking the front door. I stood at the battlement, heavy dark stone crenelations making an ideal perch. A heavy hand fell upon my neck and forced my face down. I was powerless to resist, my simulcrum was not under my control. Arms and legs flapped when I moved them, but I was bent over at the waist. "JD," I whispered.

He unprogrammed my clothes, and they went away, leaving me naked except for my jewelry. He forced his knee between mine and knocked my legs apart. I was gasping, cock jutting out directly in front of me, bracing myself for his penetration. With a laugh, he let go of me. I caught my breath, and turned around: nobody.

"Don't be invisible!" I shouted. "I hate it when you do that!"

No answer. My pulse pounded and I searched for my clothes, but couldn't find them. I shook my head, separating simulcrum from physical body, and consulted the log for my clothes' IDs, discovered they had been deleted. "Hey! You aren't supposed to delete other people's objects!" I yelled.

Damn. He was a wizard, the law. What was I going to do? Page the operators and tell 'em their boss was bothering me? How far would that get? Yeah, right.

"You're pissing me off!" I yelled.

I emailed him a rude message, "FUCK OFF AND DIE." But I didn't put my clothes back on.

I squeezed my balls, they ached with fullness, and my cock swung long and ready for the slightest touch. I needed relief, and I wanted it to be him, but I couldn't compel him. He was the better programmer. But perhaps I could seduce him.

I teleported to the fuckery. It was late, there were several couples, most of them straight, engaged in anonymous cybersex. As usual a gallery of people had gathered to watch, and with the everlasting stamina of cybersex, to participate. I walked naked into the room, selected an empty sling, climbed into it. I locked my ankles into the cuffs, feet high above the floor, scooted until my ass was placed just right for whoever wanted to fuck me. Then I locked the collar around my neck, and then my left wrist. The last cuff closed automatically on my right wrist. Now I was locked into the cuffs, and I couldn't get loose until somebody let me loose. My cock was rock hard, pointing at the sky. I didn't have long to wait, this was where the scuzzballs and deadbeats, the walking sleaze, gathered, because they knew this was where it was given away free.

The first one mounted me, and I didn't even look at him. I found myself paralyzed, listening to the patter of the computer as his program ran. I was in two spaces, the physical space my body occupied, hardon aching in my jeans, and the mental space of Cyberland where I was so immersed I was hardly aware of the computer telling me what my simulcrum was being subjected to. I felt it, even though it was only an illusion.Then my hands began to chord stream of consciousness sensations, my program sharing with everyone in the room what I was feeling, my own programming ability turning the tawdry transaction into a ball aching cyber orgy. They surrounded me, men and women, jerking off around me, stuffing cocks into my face, up my ass, splattering cum on me, reaming me endlessly. Not one of them even thought of letting me loose, I was their party favor and they used me over and over again.

All through the scene my flesh and blood ached, but I didn't touch it. I stripped off my clothes and sat naked at the console, helmet over my head, both chording balls in my hands, skin screaming for the reality of touch.

But it wasn't real, it was just cybersex. My simulcrum was screaming with lust, begging for more, and some of them were reprogramming themselves with massive pricks to fuck me. Then, as I received an impossibly large prick between my lips, I vanished.

I blinked and looked around, and found myself kneeling on straw on the floor of the stable. A leather collar was around my neck, and it was held by JDBlack. "You want a real stud, that can be arranged," he said.

I shivered. I dropped one of the chording balls and my hand went to my lap. I squeezed myself in anticipation. "Sir," I said.

He pulled on my collar, and scrambling on my knees I followed him into a stall. He clipped it to a ring in the wall, and I grabbed it. I squeezed, but the clip did not open. It was locked in programming. I teleported.

Back to the Well of Lost Souls. The place was deserted. I perched naked upon my favorite ledge. He could follow me, but would he? I had left his collar behind in the stable. I quickly chorded an early warning system, which immediately beeped and told me he was there. Invisible again. I expected no different. He was taking shameless advantage of the prerogatives of a wizard.

My simulcrum was bursting with the need to cum, and I wanted to surrender myself to the sensations of cyberlust. But I couldn't. Not without a fight. I was making myself crazy, teasing myself with JDBlack. My simulcrum masturbated, stuck a finger in its ass while jerking off, moaned and groaned, the echoes magnifying the sound. That did me in; knowing that he could hear me, hearing myself, I beat off hard and furious, wanting him to grab me by the scruff of the neck and snarl, "Take it, asshole!" and ream me.

And knowing that if he tried it, I would teleport away again.

Claws scraped stone, and I froze in mid-stroke. I dared to look over the edge of the ledge, and there, a few feet below my ledge was one of Georgie's gargoyles clawing its way up. Its eyes glowed red, and its long claws hooked into the interstices of the stone, clinging like a lizard. It had huge ears, horns, and heavy brow ridges, a flat nose and tusks. It was the size of a pony, built like a bull, moved like a dog, and hung like a horse. It resumed its climb while I watched. I couldn't move, the beast stalking me was beyond my ken. No matter how many fantasy novels I'd read, I still wasn't prepared for the creature that slithered halfway over the edge of my ledge and paused, looking at me. I rolled over onto my hands and knees and waited, sweat springing up on my brow, while it completed its climb, and placing clammy palms against my back, slid its humongous phallus against my balls. I clamped my legs shut, trapping it between them, and it was as thick as a tree branch and cold as stone. Almost I gave in, releasing it from my grasp, arching my back in anticipation—but I teleported away.

I appeared in the stable, not recollecting what destination I had chosen, mischording several keystrokes and having to redo them. But before I finished my program a match struck a sulfurous light, and JDBlack lit a lantern. The stable was dark, the door was closed. I tried to teleport, but he had placed a teleport lock on the room. Nobody could teleport in or out. I was trapped in the room with him. He stripped off his vest, revealing grey hair on his chest, his bald pate shining in the light. He unbuttoned the front of his leather jeans, converting them to chaps,

balls the size of eggs and a thick, uncut cock falling out.
He crooked his finger at me.

I stumbled to my feet and walked over to him, then
he pointed down. I dropped to my knees. I took his cock
into my mouth, hands chording spastically as I
programmed the pleasure for him. I wanted it to be good,
I wanted it to be worth all the chasing he had done. I
wanted his eyes to glaze over as he shot cum all over his
console. I wanted to win.

His hands caught my hair, and he held my head,
forcing more of his cock down my throat. I teleported
away from him. I couldn't escape the stable, but I could
still move. He materialized a length of rope and remained
standing where he was. I watched him, waiting to see
what he would do. He watched me, then his finger
crooked again. I found myself walking through a dream,
kneeling before him and looking up. He tied the rope
around my neck.

I teleported, but the rope didn't move. I was stuck in
my starting place. I jumped to my feet and backed away.
The rope stretched between us, then I was brought up
short. He tied it to a post, then yanking on the line,
brought me flying towards him. He caught me, and threw
me over the hay bales. I tried to teleport, but the rope was
a teleport lock, and it was locked to the post and my neck,
and I couldn't get out. I started desperately
programming, trying to decompile it, but he shoved his
cock into my ass, and I was too busy bucking and gasping
to program any more. Random bits of code scattered
through my throes of passion, and pinning me down with
his cock, he cleared them away.

I dropped both chording balls, stuffed several fingers
into my ass and strangled my prick with my other hand,
and jerked my physical flesh off while his program raped
my simulcrum. I splattered copious quantities of jism
across the console, but it wasn't enough.

"Please, I have to meet you in person," I begged.

He gagged my simulcrum, and I couldn't talk anymore. He savaged my ass with his prick, and I could only watch helplessly as he took total control of the scene, while my simulcrum kicked and whimpered.

At last he came, the fluids leaking from my simulcrum's asshole, which gaped open after being used so hard. I couldn't do anything at all to effect the scene. I sent him email. "Come to me in the flesh. Whoever you are, whatever you want, come and take me."

He picked up my exhausted simulcrum and led it into a stall. He fashioned bridle and reins, replacing the rope with restraints of black leather, also teleport locked. He bound my hands behind my back and hobbled my feet, and I was sunk in the reality of the cyberspace again, feeling them as if they were happening to me for real.

"You're going to stay here, my pretty boy. Going to stay here forever, ready for me to use you whenever I feel like it. You can't escape, and you're going to service me or anybody else whenever I feel like it. I shall make several keys for the stable, and lend them to friends of mine who will be invited to use you whenever they feel like it."

I nodded dumbly.

Then he blew out the lantern, leaving me in darkness. A square of light showed where he opened the door, then he was gone, the door closed behind him.

I could have deleted myself, but I didn't. It was the only way to escape the programming trap he'd put me in. Instead I enhanced his programming. I put alarms on it so I'd know when he was there.

It's only Cyberland, nothing is real, it's a complicated game of make believe played by programmers who push each other's abilities to the limits, exploiting each other's sexuality for prurient gratification. It isn't real, none of it, not one bit, but every time the alarm whispers his name, I drop what I'm doing and grab my chording balls, ready to submit to his desires.

Guernica

M. Christian

By the flatscreen on the wall, it was just past the 21st century. Glowing numerals flickered into 13:00: late enough for the mischief-makers. The cops were still rolling through the city outside, but just maybe a bit lethargic; reptiles chocked full 'a donuts and acid coffee. The bribes to the neighbors were paid and the acoustics, as always, were perfect—the people on Wake street hoped

13:01 and the little house on Wake street changed. Tension sang through the building; time to play. Outside, the forces of legislated morality motored about—but here, inside, out came the toys. The crowd's change was hard, precise: slaves shrugged off civilian personas and dropped their eyes as masters closed steel-gray attitudes over theirs. The private home with eyebolts, heavily upholstered chairs and mysterious trunks, changed: chains were hung, and straps of nasty leather were clipped to tables.

The trunks revealed their contents: highly illegal latex, rubber, dildoes, lubrication, handcuffs, whips, clothespins, canes, condoms, dams, gloves, and other toys. The clock was 13:15—and then it blipped right over to a tape: Mistress Gloria flagellating a slave. His bed sheet-white ass was striped, welts like red-hot prison bars across his cheeks. He smiled back to the crowd from the screen from the past when he wasn't a criminal, and what he was doing wasn't a Morality Crime. Now, in the years around 13:15, his stripes could land his ass in jail, or in one of the mining camps, and just viewing the tape could do the same to the people of the Wake Street house.

The cane in the video mistress' hand descended. It was a good quality copy: you could see the slight curve of the white birch rod as it bent to the slope of the slave's ass, the subtle breath of its passing, and the slightly wet kiss of wood to—was that blood? Were those streaks redder than usual welts? Did that rod suddenly have a lipstick streak of the bottom's liquid contents? A very good video. Forget jail, owning this was a one-way ticket to gray hair and hard labor—if you survived interrogation—and all of the pain non-negotiated, not consensual. And all the gay rape you could ever want.

The bottom on the screen became a metronome to the proceedings. Whack! Street clothes put away, play clothes came out. Whack! Sudden glimpses of sweat-glimmering thighs, breasts, backs, cheeks, tight chests, chalky skin (the sun never properly introduced to these regions: nudity = jail). Whack! A redhead with ribs in evidence and breasts that would rattle in a cupped hand, bent to pull on regulation boots, her sex flowering open behind her—and triggering a chorus of salivation from the opposite side of the room. Whack! A buzz-cut, he-man tugged on regulation prison sweats, the neck and head of his cock catching, then vanishing, past the draw-strings with a rubbery nod. Those on that side of the room returned the nod, smiling. A comfortable man with a warm, soft chest buckled on his official web belt and pinned a fake badge to his shirt. His eyes followed, with a tightening and flexing of ass, a short man with tumbleweed-wild hair, who absently tightened and flexed his gloves.

Enforcement Officers patrolled the city outside: tight beams of searing light punching visibility in the darkness, always, perpetually, without sleep (for their sign was a wide-awake, watchful eye) searching for crime, theft, murder, vandalism, vagrancy, ill-morality, perversion, homosexuality, sex, affection, less or more than nuclear familiarity, or enjoyment.

The clock was still gone, still replaced by the prison-bar streaked submissive, but they all knew, felt, that it was time to start: two lines, submissives on one side— quaking in their thin-soled prison shoes (copied with great care from the real thing) against one wall; dominants on the other—flexing leather gloves or fondling toys (copied with great care from the real thing, used by those that patrolled outside). The clock couldn't show it, but they all knew it was party time—time to arrest and be arrested by the forces of fear and punishment—ah, but safety, consensually.

Some of the submissives had their ankles chained, the links making heavy music on the hardwood floor. The excitement level in the room rose a few notches, and following right behind was a darkside excitement; maybe someone would hear, maybe someone would call the cops, maybe they'd spend the rest of their lives in chains, maybe they'd be beaten, probably they'd die. The fear made simple play into terror play.

There was some hesitancy on the part of the dominants. A spice of suspense for the submissives? No one wanting to start? What was that noise outside?

Then officer George approached prisoner #16 (Caucasian male, 25-28 years old, brown curly hair-short cut, no tattoos or scars). Hooking a sausage finger into a convenient D-ring, the officer hauled the prisoner to his knees and pressed 16's face hard into the leather-resistance of his government issued (a copy) crotchguard. "Breathe," he commanded.

The submissive did as instructed, breath squeaking through leather-pressed nostrils.

"Bet it's getting hard," growled the fascist pretender.

The submissive nodded, rubbing his nose (his breathing changed tone) on the hard leather.

Then the officer pulled a pair of handcuffs from his belt, ratcheted them on #16's wrist and then to his own belt. Then he did it again, with another pair of cuffs, another wrist, the other side of the belt.

"How strong are your teeth?" Officer George growled.

#16 dug out the zipper with his lips and teeth and feasted on the condomed cock he found hard and waiting.

A portrait of officer Lawrence hard at work (done in hard Weegee light, high contrast, gritty, realistic—the untied shoelace, the pistol hanging obviously in the way, the dusty floor, the plaster wall scarred and dented): It'd taken him a few minutes to get into position—and the same went for the target: Lawrence's feet were apart, his arm was back, his fist was clenched, his knuckles were white, his shirt was sweat-stained, his face strained, and his eyes gleamed with feverish concentration.

The whip in his hand was obviously heavy; his wrist was hurting—you could see it in his eyes.

The target was just something officer Lawrence could hit, it wasn't important—just a bullseye in felt marker on a pimpled asscheek, that usual ecstatic glazed expression, those runs of welts—they'd all seen his like a thousand times before

It was the joy Lawrence obviously put into his job that made the picture special.

The body-cavity search Officer Laura was conducting was going well. So far she'd been able to remove the thirty five cents (two dimes, ten pennies, one nickel) from prison #3's ass without having to resort to the enema nozzle hanging next to prisoner #8, Tayle, Sally, Q.

That didn't mean, though, that she wouldn't need it eventually.

Officer Goby interrogated prisoner #12:
    "What kind of animal are you?"
    "I'm a fuck-beast sir."
    "What the fuck's that?"
    "I live to get screwed, sir."
    "Get screwed by what, cunt?"
    "Anything that moves, sir."
    "Well, I'm not goin' ta fuck ya."
    "You're not, sir?"
    "You're butt-fuck ugly, I don't fuck shit that's buttfuck ugly."
    "Am I ugly, sir?"
    "Ugly as shit. Why'd you come here, anyway?"
    "To get fucked, sir."
    "Well you ain't gonna get fucked—too buttfuck ugly. I don't fuck buttfuck ugly."
    "What do you with ugly, sir?'
    "I beat the crap out of it."
    And so officer's belt met transvestite's pantied ass— and Officer Goby's hitting was really pretty—not buttfuck ugly, not at all.

Prisoner #2 was a vaporous man, all pale skin and blue veins, standing, shivering, in one corner. He was an alabaster rail, a naked beanpole.

Officer Eigan was bold, bearded and hair: a golden bear from some technological forest—he seemed pretty adapt with the hypodermic, amphlets, scalpels, and razors he absently fondled.

... and in one corner a soft, slow, (like the slowly menacing gears of some great machine) a gang bang was going on—the sex of the lust object in it was lost to conjecture and distant memory.

... on a sling a female prisoner had her public hygiene inspected by a iron-plated dyke, the clamps and chains on her tits making a windchime backup to her moaning.

... in a corner two bad boys roughhoused themselves into a squishing doggie-style fuck.

... tied to the points of the compass on the floor, a knotted prisoner's ass slowly ripened under the constant beating four officers gave it with cane, cat, paddle, and whip (in that order).

... spread over a vaulting horse, a great titted redhead cried tears of near-orgasmic joy at the skilled licks of her tiny-titted partner.

... from an iron-barred cage an electronic buzzing and the sting of ozone filled the air—the ongoing torture of a soft, pale prisoner for not doing an adequate Gene Kelly impression. A jolt of current came to his nipples and scrotum with every criticism of his very lackluster soft-shoe

... one couple, he with a cock, she with a cunt, plugged into each other with a feverish abandon while each, sporting high-tech claws, painted the other with stripes of slowly drippng blood.

And so on, and on, and no, into the night. The clock never moved from the prison-barred ass (but by this time the

VCD had been played a half-dozen times) but dawn was threatening none the less.

Camp was broken, toys put away, uniforms balled up (or anally folded to regulation standards in the case of those that had gone deep into character), deep breaths taken, nerves steadied, thanks given, taken, dates made, coats buttoned—and out they went.

And, to a player, a distant, predictable thought crossed their minds like a distant mental fright train: that beyond the front door, down the street, on the corner, at work, at their homes, could be the crisp precision of an arrest. Prison. The Camps. Death.

They left—excited beyond any play they had done, could do—into real terror.

Form
Pagan O'Leary

I paused outside the doors to the auditorium. Inside, the staff and students were ready to begin the ceremony and yet all would wait on my arrival. No one would murmur, "where is he?" No one would later question me on my tardiness. Standing in the silent spotless hallway, I felt the weight of the time I was demanding of them, and the sheer pleasure of it made me shudder.

I have imposed order on chaos, civilized the primitive savage and taught it to dress with elegance, and in return been yielded this power. I do not take it lightly. To the contrary, I savor and cherish their respect, their deference. It isn't selfishness. When I make them wait, their anticipation is heightened and the eventual satisfaction is only increased by the waiting. Even in the exercise of my authority, I serve their needs.

As one, they rose to their feet at my entrance, motionless until I reached my seat on stage. My senior trainer Aragon stepped forward and I relaxed into the soothing flow of formalities.

Aragon's voice was mellifluous as she began calling the names. "Darrell Lothbein, to be known as Rezor." Cocky in his new leathers, the graduate sauntered across the stage. I noticed Aragon speak to him quietly as she presented the certificate that symbolized the amendment to his license earned by his completion of our course. Ever conscientious, she permitted no lapses in standards, even at this final moment. The new dominant bowed in acknowledgement and left the stage with evident humility; I nodded in satisfaction.

"Angela Boone, to be known as Tory." As the slow parade continued, I surveyed our audience. They sat grouped in their classes, easily identifiable to the practiced eye. Our basic students were noticeably younger than the rest, wide eyed and uncomfortable and fascinated. Graduation was the only occasion when they were permitted to leave their secluded classroom. Aragon sometimes suggests we lessen the segregation.

"We give them a glimpse of the possibilities at graduation," I explain to her each time. "But they don't even have their basic license yet—they haven't earned the right to be part of the greater mysteries." She never argues, and in recognition of that courtesy I permit her to repeat her request at intervals. It has nearly become a private ritual for us.

The bi class could be those same basics five years later, bracketed by the gay male and gay female, and behind them the polys. Seating for graduation isn't dictated, but somehow the orientation classes all herd together as if by instinct, separating themselves from the alternatives.

I have little to do with the orientation half of the school, preferring to leave its management to Ananda, a sweet polybi who delights in the baby steps of sexuality. Orientation keeps us solvent; in my mind, the heart of the school is the alternatives. I smiled over at that side of the room. There the groups mingled, the fetishists and bodmods, the voyeurs and tvs, the freeminded, the adventurous. My people.

And directly below me, my jewels—dominants in training, carefully dignified in their stark black uniforms, a semicircle of submissives kneeling at their feet, the beginners shivering in newly issued white tunics.

As the final graduate left the stage, I rose and walked forward. I give the same speech each time, grandiose and portentous. The words need no meaning; only the impact of sounds and sight and atmosphere linger, and so I create for them a profound memory to treasure. Even after years, when I chance upon an old student—they remember me, I seldom remember them—it is sure to be mentioned: "Your speech was so inspiring, Professor, I've never forgotten it."

Only the graduates bowed properly as I exited the stage and moved toward the door. Some of the new students showed the initiative to ape them, albeit awkwardly, and the orientation students who lack these respectful formalities in their lovestyles merely stood uncertainly. But one bright-eyed sub lowered her forehead to the floor in a graceful obeisance. I murmured approvingly as I passed her and knew the others would note it, perhaps discover they wanted to earn it for themselves. It was a very good morning.

The satisfaction stayed with me to my office, even when Cilla followed behind me and knelt beside my desk. I frowned in mock exasperation. "Time for reports again, little nag?"

Cilla was too discreet to sigh in relief at my good humor—after all, she'd trained here at our school, taking every course for which she qualified before hiring on to become my assistant -but I sensed the easing of her tension as she nodded her head toward my monitor.

I glanced at the display of names and numbers. Today's graduating class. I signed my name to the screen then traded Cilla the stylus for the keyboard and typed in the password that would verify my signature.

"Strip to the waist," I commanded with a soft chuckle when she would have forwarded to the next report and was pleased to startle her. I'm seldom playful when dealing with mundane details of the school, though

I fuss more out of boredom than true dislike. This is how we survive, after all, providing the training required for licensing. In turn, the government and insurance companies pay—but only when the reports are done.

Cilla blushed deliciously as she released the shoulder tabs of her tunic, letting the thin material drape around her waist. I played with her heavy breasts for a few minutes, cupping and squeezing their warm weight, then pinching the nipples lightly until they came obediently firm. I leaned back, considering, then nodded. "Yes. I like that. Next report?"

This was one of Cilla's delights, being used or exposed in some sweetly humiliating manner while conducting business as usual. A lovely shiver ran through her as she leaned toward the keyboard. I grinned at her until she lowered her eyes meekly, then I reluctantly returned my attention to the display. More routine— certification of attendance for the new students, authorizing them mental wellness leave from their jobs. Another signature, another password.

"Wider." I nudged one thigh gently then smacked it when she responded too slowly. Cilla giggled. I slapped the other thigh and laughed with her. "Now tell me about the next report," I instructed her. As I slid my fingers between her legs to test her wetness, she gasped and stammered about scene name registrations, her words fading to whimpers as I pinched and tugged the swollen lips.

We finished the remainder without hurry since I paused between each one to torment the sub at my feet. She was bristling with clamps and moaning audibly when Aragon entered.

Taking a seat, she plugged in her notebook and began a staccato dance of fingers across her keyboard without appearing to notice us. In anyone else, I would have thought it polite discretion, but from my senior trainer it was merely indifference.

I finished my game and swatted Cilla's bottom to send her crawling from the office. Without looking up, Aragon said briskly, "Class profile."

I studied the file she'd brought up on my screen, then growled. "Nearly half of the doms are new here."

"You'll see that happening more now with the publicity you've been getting. Why should they settle for a correspondence course and practical at a clinic when they can come here?"

"They've had no sub training." I glared at her and she shrugged.

"Not required by law. If you set it as policy, we'll lose our funding." She repeated her lines with some boredom. Aragon was occasionally impatient with my vision.

It was compromises such as this that sometimes made me regret entering this business. This school was my dream, and I prided myself on creating a place of elegance and tradition. I demanded more of my students than any other school, though dozens had sprung up in the larger cities to mimic my concept of providing basic through pansexual education in one interlocking framework. A certificate from the Professor was prized in the public Clubs and Houses. But I even was hamstrung by regulation, forced to accept any applicant who passed the psych evals.

We scanned through the individual profiles quickly. Their immediate trainers would review them in depth, noting emotional triggers and potential danger points, all neatly quantified and labeled by the examining clinics. I make it a practice to look at each one myself as well, though, knowing my years of experience may sometimes mark what a bored technician with only a het monog license might overlook.

"This one," I announced firmly, freezing the screen before Aragon could flash past it. "She has true potential. Did you see her in the auditorium as I left?"

"Raw talent, Professor? Or perhaps just another hopeful who's read books she's not licensed to buy yet?"

My jaw tightened at her acerbic comment. I motioned silently for her to continue the scroll.

Aragon is the only other staff member with a pansexual license and thus within the school is second only to me. I've observed her training techniques and grant that she is somehow able to coax the frightened and shrink the bullies and lure the wary, but toward me she is always aloof and detached, a guise that turns me cold. We work well together, yet much time in her company sends me fleeing for the soft laughing warmth of Cilla.

Or, as now, to the training rooms. Leaving Aragon to review the rest of the profiles, I headed for one of the domination classes. Shiva halted the exercise that the students could bow when I entered, then slapped her crop against her boot in signal to resume as I took a seat to one side.

The students were paired off, the one acting in place of the sub stripped and bound to a frame. The doms were practicing with floggers. Faces set in grim concentration, they stood waiting as Shiva established a rhythm with the crop against her boot, raising their arms in unison as she gave the command to begin.

I closed my eyes, lulled by the monotonous thump of leather on skin. "Increase the impact, not the speed," I heard Shiva hiss as she moved slowly across the room. "No, your pattern is too routine. Be regular but random."

The thuds began to echo in the room, a mesmerizing tempo. The silence between strokes was pushed aside by the heavy breathing of the working students and the sighing moans of those being pleasured. Our doms experienced everything they learned to inflict before they left us, and even the most obdurately dominant usually admitted to enjoying the floggings.

Shiva halted the class. "Are your partners aroused?" Peering around through half-opened eyes, I was amused at the looks of bewilderment. The usual pattern. "This is not batting practice, boys and girls," Shiva lectured with derision. "You must observe. Learn your partner's reactions. This is a dance for two." I slipped quietly from the room as she instructed them to untie and rub down their partners before switching.

Calmer now, I entered the adjoining room. Siesta smiled in delight as I entered and whispered hurriedly to the small group of submissives kneeling in a circle around her. As one, they rose and curtsied gracefully, the men performing a modified bow, and then with a rush I was surrounded. Chuckling softly, I allowed them to seat me. They moved quickly but with grace, lifting my feet to a comfortable hassock, a cool drink appearing at my hand, a thin pillow being placed behind my neck.

"Well done." I toasted Siesta, and she dimpled pleasingly.

"We were just discussing the pleasures of serving, Professor. You have impeccable timing."

I relaxed and allowed Siesta to make me part of her lesson. One student massaged my shoulders while two others removed my shoes and leisurely bathed and pampered my feet. Siesta selected her best student for the privilege of curling up in my lap to stroke and caress me with soft hands and warm lips. The rest she put through their paces, drilling them in positions and responses for my approval. Eager and beautiful, they restored my good humour.

I waited a few days before checking in on the new subs. The lectures and discussions that began their training were essential, but a bit dull for my taste. I joined them on the third day as Vizier was unlocking the toyboxes.

"For the next hour, I want you to explore," he announced after leading the group in acknowledging my entrance. "Play, see what items interest you."

The students quickly lost their self consciousness as they became engrossed in their playtime, donning cuffs and collars, testing clamps, gingerly using paddles on each other. I looked for Angie, the woman I'd noted the first day, and found her kneeling quietly by her assigned toybox, removing the items from it and laying them neatly on the floor in front of her.

My attention drifted until I heard a loud, firm "No!" One of the students was leaning over Angie dangling a thick rubber gag in front of her face. Vizier joined them and took the gag from the embarrassed student.

"Have you ever worn a gag?" the trainer asked Angie quietly. She shook her head, her mouth stubbornly clenched tight. "I want you to try it on. You can put it on yourself, no one will touch you." She shook her head again, glancing at me then dropping her eyes. Vizier motioned to me and we withdrew to his office where we could talk privately while still observing the class through the window.

Vizier had no need to consult me, of course. My policies forbid ever forcing a student to do anything, even though on admission they agreed to offer complete obedience and consented to punishment if the school felt it necessary. And of course there was the prospect of failing to complete the course, losing their chance for the license. We would neither force Angie nor punish her; but she could see us from the classroom, stern and disapproving as we pretended to discuss her failure to obey, and perhaps that would spur her to attempt the gag.

Vizier recalled a joke and so it was several minutes before I glanced through the window and noticed smugly that the black rubber gag was now fastened around her head. Her cheeks were damp with tears. I felt a rush at her surrender in order to please us and motioned to the trainer.

"Submission is not doing what you want to do," a familiar voice was saying as we reentered the classroom. Vizier stumbled into me as I stopped abruptly in shock. "It's wanting to do what you're told—whatever that might be."

I pushed my way through the students. "Eric."

He barely glanced at me. "Kurt. I was just convincing this little pet she likes being gagged." He knelt down beside her and gripped her hair, tugging her head back as he smiled down at her. He slipped his other hand beneath her tunic. "You like to please me, don't you?" he coaxed, his voice seductive velvet as his hand moved on her, and to my dismay she nodded even as the tears spilled again, and she arched her hips forward.

"Vizier, ungag her," I barked. I could feel my hands trembling with restrained anger. "Eric—my office."

I sent Cilla to find Aragon and paced my office waiting.

Eric sauntered in casually and walked straight up to me, holding out his hand, smiling. "Kurt, it's good to see you again." I could only stare at him, so nonchalant as if he had no doubts of his welcome. Shrugging, he lowered his hand and leaned against the wall. "You look old, Kurt."

He didn't look old, though we were close in age. His hair was long and shaggy with no hint of grey, creating a decade of difference next to my carefully trimmed black and silver mane. His face was tan and barely lined, his time in jail apparently not marking him at all. I thought bitterly of my deepening wrinkles, the growing slump to my shoulders and belly.

I snorted and walked away, taking a seat behind my desk. "What do you want, Eric? You're not supposed to be on the premises."

Why shouldn't I come here?" Eric asked in surprise. "It's my school too."

"I'll buy you out."

"No, I don't think so," he drawled thoughtfully, staring at me intently. His eyes seemed more silver than blue now, paler than I remembered. "I'll admit that I hate what you've made of it but I'm not ready to sell."

"The court ordered you to stay away," I reminded him. He held up a finger to stop me, a familiar impish grin creasing his face, then reached in his pocket and tugged out a license, tossing it on the desk in front of me. I stared at it in disbelief, at the distinctive bold P beneath the medical clearance. "It's not real." Forging and selling licenses had been one of Eric's crimes.

"It's real, Kurt. I'm a licensed pansexual. What do you think, should I start as a trainer?"

"No!" I'd shoved back the chair and was halfway around the desk before I realized I intended to hit him. How long since I'd been provoked to violence? Glaring, I stopped and stood facing him, determined to protect the school from whatever threat he might pose.

Eric hadn't moved. Arms folded across his chest, he sighed and shook his head. "Don't be a fool. I'm not coming back. I couldn't stand a day here." Dropping his arms to his sides, he approached me slowly. "Do you remember what it was like, Kurt?" he asked softly, wrapping his fingers into the front of my shirt, pulling me toward him. "When did you last feel passion? The last time you screamed? I used to make you scream, Kurt, I made you beg and plead for me to fuck you, remember?"

His face was so close, the low taunting voice racing through my ears to enflame my body.

And to my horror I realized that for a moment, I wanted him to use me again. That timbre in his voice, the challenge in that tight grasp, the heat of his breath on my face, all combined to taunt my control. It was a moment of temptation yet the sordid allure of it was enough to strengthen my resolve.

Ignoring the warm weakness oozing through my legs, I removed his hand from my shirt with a semblance of calm. I returned to my chair and noticed Aragon standing in the doorway.

"Eric? You came back." Pale and flustered, her voice shaking, she held her fists pressed tightly to her belly as if staunching a wound.

"You know him?" I hadn't hired Aragon until after Eric's trial, had hired her to replace him in fact.

Eric raised his eyebrow sardonically, still watching me steadily. "She's mine, Kurt. That's why I'm here, to get her. I suppose she didn't tell you—being owned by an outlaw wouldn't enhance her resume." He gestured to Aragon. She didn't move, and he glanced at her curiously before shrugging.

"This school is a mockery," he continued quietly, turning back toward me. "The whole system is a joke. Deciding who can have sex, when, how —rules and regulations for something that should be wild and untamed. Look at you, Kurt—strutting the halls with pretensions to godhood because you can make people bow to you —virginal medieval manners taking the place of lust and heat. You're pathetic."

I snorted in disgust. His antisocial philosophies had only worsened. We had worked together once, loved together, finding ways to educate the curious even before it could be done openly. But Eric had hated it when sexual health finally achieved a respectability. His rebelliousness had nearly lost us the school.

Aragon remained frozen, expressionless. Had she really belonged to my fiery partner, this coldly efficient, phlegmatic trainer of mine? I couldn't picture it. Nor, for all our slight disagreements over time, could I picture her turning her back on the ideals of the school. She hadn't joined him when he beckoned.

"Sex is too important to be left to the ignorant," I countered stubbornly, though I knew I'd never convince him. "They learn safety here, and self- acceptance. No more fumbling with unrecognized desires, no more shame, no more hiding. This is freedom for us, Eric, not tyranny."

"No," he said softly, shaking his head. "Let me show you what you've forgotten."

Eric took Aragon's hand and led her unprotesting to a chair facing my desk. She moved stiffly, only her eyes alive as they darted frantically from his face to mine, but she didn't protest. And I watched, strangely reluctant to interfere, briefly feeling again his hand possessively gripping my shirt.

She sat at his command, meeting my eyes as he stood behind her. He rested both hands on the back of the chair, not touching her, watching me.

His voice was hot brown sugar, sweet and heavy, slowly melting into the cracks of my mind. He spoke through her to me, showing me her body. I could see behind the clothes she wore, see the changes as his words stroked her. Her skin was coming to life, the nerves tingling in anticipation of more ghostly verbal caresses. She didn't shift in the chair but I could feel her urge to move and make the too tenuous touches real. I felt the same urge and forced myself still, unwilling to give him any reaction.

He knew. "You want to move now," he said, deep voice close to her ear. "You feel him watching you and you know he sees you now as I do, open and helpless. But you can't move until I let you. It isn't his eyes you want, it isn't his touch, and you have no choice but to let him look. Put your hands behind your neck."

For an instant, I heard it as a command for me and lowered my hands to the chair arms in chagrin, hoping he hadn't seen. I gritted my teeth.

Such a slight change in position and such a stunning affect on Aragon, now hungry eyed and breathing heavily, her face tense with the effort to hide her responses. "He hasn't touched you yet but suppose I told him to? Yes...suppose I call him over here and tell him to stroke your breasts, to feel how they've tightened with excitement. And he will feel your nipples hard against his fingertips begging to be fondled and pinched and twisted. Perhaps I'll tell him to taste them and bite them—you don't want him nursing on you, but there's nothing you can do, is there? No choice."

He was teasing me, tormenting me. Relentless he detailed the pain and pleasure he could have me inflict on her under his instruction, coaxing our minds to deceive our bodies. My cock was erect and throbbing. I'd never wanted her before but she was so damn vulnerable bound to that chair as surely as if he'd tied her with rope. I could see myself dragging my hands, my teeth, my cock, across her reluctant flesh, and it wouldn't be me doing it because Eric would be siphoning his desire through my body. He didn't touch her but she squirmed in the chair, whimpering now as he worked her deeper. So aroused, I doubt her staring eyes even saw me anymore. And I, I was still in my chair while I was crawling all over her ferocious and rough and ravenous.

He touched her, spreading her legs wide and yanking her skirt up to her hips, and she gasped loudly masking my own involuntary moan. Lulled by the fragile spell of illusion, reality stunned with its intensity. Eric growled in her ear, taunting her, and I was poised desperately for him to complete the command. I saw it just as he was described, how he would hold her in the chair and feed her to me, drown me with her juices. I could taste it in his words, in her frantic eyes. Then as he held her for me, we would take her, hot and deep and ruthless while she struggled beneath us. We watched her fight us, felt it, and we kept ramming into her body in a wild heat.

Grabbing her hair, he yanked her head back. "Come for me," he commanded and he stole her cries from me with a brutal kiss. I could only watch as she writhed and bucked against the chair, so far from me, so distant, and he gave me nothing. No command, no touch, no release.

Eric raised his head finally, watching me sternly as he held her flushed face against him, stroking her hair. "What does this have to do with anything you teach here?" he asked quietly.

Suddenly I was reminded of where we were and felt myself shrinking inside. He'd tricked me again.

"I run a House," he said conversationally, lifting Aragon from the chair and helping her adjust her clothing as she clung to his arm. "It's not registered, Kurt, you'll never find us. But don't think we're not still out there in the shadows. Some of us will never accept the leash of laws, no matter how it's disguised to be for our own good."

"What if she doesn't want to go?" I demanded out as he reached for the door. Chuckling, he held her tightly to him.

"Kurt, she consented to me. Consent is given to a person, not an act. And so she made her choice—the rest are mine."

The little sub Angie was standing on the other side of the door when he opened it, and she dropped to her knees immediately. I wondered dully how long she'd listened.

"I want to go with you," she said shyly, twisting her hands and staring at Eric's boots. "The way you made me submit in class....it felt so right. Please, take me with you."

I rolled my eyes in disgust. What next? Was he going to play Pied Piper and seduce the whole school to his feet? At least he had the courtesy not to laugh at her even as he shook his head.

"I'll leave this one with you, Kurt," he called over his shoulder as he guided Aragon around the kneeling woman. "But she'll find us someday. They all will."

The footsteps faded. They were gone. Silly Angie was staring at me with tears in her eyes. "He was a Master, wasn't he, Professor?" she whispered.

I quoted from the manual: "Slavery is an ancient historical concept that often finds its way into fantasy role-playing, but in reality there are no—" Too pompous. Too predictable. I touched the front of my shirt, remembering.

She wasn't listening anyway. I sighed. "Yes. He was a Master."

Contributors

Gary Bowen is a queer writer of Apache/Welsh descent, originally from Texas, now living on the East Coast. He has published over 200 stories in anthologies and magazines and is the author of *Diary of a Vampire*, *Man Hungry*, and *Queer Destinies*. His work appears in numerous other Circlet Press anthologies. His web site can be visited at www.netgsi.com/~fcowboy

Lauren P. Burka's works appear in several anthologies published by Circlet Press, as well as Laura Antoniou's *By Her Subdued*, and Susie Bright's *Best American Erotica*. Despite her tarot cards' prediction, she now has a day job. Ms. Burka presently resides in Cambridge, Massachusetts with her pets, human and otherwise.

Renée M. Charles' work has appeared in *Best American Erotica 1995*, *Dark Angels*, *Blood Kiss*, *Selling Venus*, *Symphonie's Gift* and other erotic anthologies and magazines in the last couple of years. When not writing erotica, she tends to her multi-cat "family." She is single and has a B.S. in English.

M. Christian's stories have appeared in such anthologies as *Best American Erotica 1994* and *1997*, *Best Gay Erotica*, the *Mammoth Book of Historical Erotica*, *Noirotica 1 2 & 3*, and, from Circlet Press, *More Technosex*, *Selling Venus*, *Wired Hard Vol. 2*, and *Genderflex*. He also edited the anthologies *Eros Ex Machina*, *Midsummer Nights Dreams*, and *Guilty Pleasures*. He is also a world renowned perv—more than anything because it allows him to combine his two favorite activities: sex and shopping.

Reina Delacroix is the pen name of a shy, quiet librarian, living in Northern Virginia with her cats, George and Shen T'ien; her precious Pet, Michael; and her loyal Wolf, Marc. This is her fifth story to see print with Circlet Press.

Neal Harkness makes his Circlet Press debut with this story.

Andrea J. Horlick is a health-care professional and writer of dark fiction, poetry, and erotica. She spends far too much time online arguing about the few things she knows and the many things on which she has an opinion. She has always been a little twisted and perverse but is just now beginning to get paid for it.

Raven Kaldera is a mythical beast come to life, a transgendered intersexual leatherpagan minister, farmer, and parent who writes twisted erotica in order to change the world and carry out an agenda of perversion and enlightenment. You have been warned.

Michael Manning, cover artist, is the artist and creator of the graphic novels *The Spider Garden*, *Hydrophidian*, and *Cathexis*. A collection of his graphic images, *Lumenagerie*, was also published by NBM. His most recent work is a graphic novel also from NBM entitled *Tranceptor* (in collaboration with artist Patrick Conlon).

Pagan O'Leary says "After twenty itinerant years in the military, I've finally found a home in the Pacific

Northwest. I play with computers and write technical materials in the daytime, and play with computers and write fiction at night. My other hobbies include leathercrafting, costuming, reading, and bellydance."

R. L. Perkins is an aerospace engineer living in the Delaware Valley in a bigamous relationship with a computer and a cat. When not trapped on airplanes he spends most of his free time hanging out in a bohemian coffee house in Philadelphia. "Local Reference" is his second story to see print in a Circlet Press publication.

Jason Rubis' fiction, poetry and articles have appeared in *Aberrations, Variations, Leg Show, The Seattle Weekly,* and *Industrial Decay Quarterly.* Jason Rubis lives and works in Washington, D.C.

About the Editor

Photo by Efrain Gonzalez

Cecilia Tan, editor, has edited over thirty volumes of erotic science fiction and fantasy for Circlet Press, the company she founded in 1992. She is the author of *Black Feathers: Erotic Dreams,* a collection of SM-themed erotic short stories published in 1998 by HarperCollins Publishers, and *The Velderet: A Cybersex S/M Serial,* forthcoming from Circlet Press. Her work can be found in magazines from *Penthouse* to *Ms.,* and anthologies like *Best American Erotica 1996* and *Eros Ex Machina.*

Acknowledgements

We would like to thank all the very patient people out there who waited so long for this book. Thanks to the significant others of the contributors for supporting our artistic addictions. Special thanks to John for technological patronage, Susan for dedicated editorial service, and Circlet's inimitable brigade of interns for everything under the sun. Felice, for being in the trenches with us, Mitch & Gerrie for continual support, and of course everyone at LPC for never giving up.

More Hot Stuff from Circlet Press

October 1999

Sexcrime: Subversive Erotica
edited by Cecilia Tan

A woman performs S/M on a futuristic stage where all sensual pain must be faked. A man searches for a secret sex "speakeasy" in a high tech city. An assassin finds herself irresistibly attracted to her victim. An artist's model poses in a world where erotic expression is taboo. A catastrophe releases the inhibitions of people to do more than riot and loot.

Taking its title from 1984, George Orwell's dystopian novel, Sexcrime explores the erotic heat and intensity that can breed under repressive conditions.

June 1999

S/M Futures: Millenium Edition
edited by Cecilia Tan

First published in 1995, when most of its contributors were virtual unknowns and the millenium seemed distant, S/M Futures was the first anthology to explore the cutting edge of sex and erotic fiction by combining science fiction and kink. In 1999, we find the future is here today.

The new edition features an introduction by Laura Antoniou, and an all new story by Cecilia Tan.

More Hot Stuff from Circlet Press

November 1999

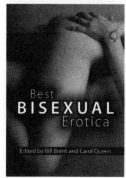

Best Bisexual Erotica
edited by Carol Queen & Bill Brent

What is bisexual erotica? You'll find out in this Best Of anthology, compiled by San Francisco's sexiest editors, Carol Queen (author of *Exhibitionism for the Shy* and *The Leather Daddy and the Femme*) and Bill Brent (editor of *Black Sheets* magazine).

The first volume in this ground-breaking new series, *Best Bisexual Erotica* presents some of the finest, hottest cutting edge fiction being written today.

June 1999

The Velderet: A Cybersex S/M Serial
written by Cecilia Tan

Bellonia is a peaceful utopia of a world where "inequality" is taboo. But that leaves our heroes, Merin and Kobi, unfulfilled. For these two roommates share a secret obsession: the playing of master/slave sex games. Their sexuality becomes the key to their world's survival, though, when conquerors from another world arrive.

Originally published as a serial in *Taste of Latex* Magazine, *The Velderet* ran for six issues before the magazine folded. Find out now what happens in the end!

Order These Titles Now From Circlet Press!

Beyond Vanilla
TALES FROM THE EROTIC EDGE: A CIRCLET OMNIBUS, EDITED BY CECILIA TAN, $15.95
A fat 272 page volume collecting four Circlet books into one: *Telepaths Don't Need Safewords* by Cecilia Tan, *Mate* by Lauren P. Burka, *Feline Fetishes*, edited by corwin & *Forged Bonds*, edited by Cecilia Tan. With a decided S/M edge, kinky and different.

Celebrate Sex
SEXMAGICK: WOMEN CONJURING EROTIC FANTASY, EDITED BY CECILIA TAN, $7.95
Stories where magic is real, myth is erotic, and sex is power. Every story combines ritual and mystery to make sex transformative, erotic power that breaks curses, renews life, and heals.

SEXMAGICK 2: MEN CONJURING EROTIC FANTASY, EDITED BY CECILIA TAN, $9.95
More stories of erotic magic, this time by mostly male authors. Rituals of everlasting passion? You bet.

EARTHLY PLEASURES, BY REED MANNING, $9.95
Reed Manning has thrilled the readers of men's magazines for years with his combinations of sci-fi and hot sex. For the first time, the best of his fiction is in one book. "These are pleasurable stories about people seeking pleasure."
    —Jack C. Haldeman II

SELLING VENUS: FUTURISTIC SEX WORK TALES, EDITED BY CECILIA TAN, $9.95
Hot stories envision future call girls, exotic dancers, and forms of sex work not yet invented... as only science fiction writers can.

Les/Bi/Gay/Trans
WIRED HARD 2: MORE EROTICA FOR A GAY UNIVERSE, EDITED BY C. TAN, $14.95
Homoerotic, futuristic stories populated by fighter pilots, high tech detectives, interstellar diplomats, prison convicts, espionage agents, and even angels, all men who love men. Dark, gritty, the stories in Wired Hard 2 go deep into the psyche of male-male eroticism. With stories by Gary Bowen, M. Christian, Tom Dickson, Mason Powell, and more.

WIRED HARD: EROTICA FOR A GAY UNIVERSE, EDITED BY C. TAN, $7.95
The first volume in the Wired Hard series. Male authors including Mason Powell, Gary Bowen, Leo Scott and David Laurents present erotica that is truly "out of this world."

THE NEW WORLDS OF WOMEN: SAPPHIC SF EROTICA, EDITED BY CECILIA TAN, $10.95
Eleven stories of women who love women, including six brand new tales! "Fantasy and science fiction can inspire erotica that stretches the imagination... the *New Worlds of Women* proves it."—Lambda Book Report

GENDERFLEX: SEXY STORIES ON THE EDGE & IN BETWEEN, EDITED BY CECILIA TAN, $12.95
12 tales that twist, blur, break, or bend gender roles with magic, science, and dreams.

The Erotic Vampire Series

CHERISHED BLOOD, EDITED BY CECILIA TAN, $14.95
The third book in this series of hot anthologies mixing vampires and erotica in a dark and delicious fashion. Cherished Blood is about 1/3 lesbian, 1/3 gay, and 1/3 het in focus, and all sexy, sensual tales of blood lust.

BLOOD KISS: VAMPIRE EROTICA EDITED BY CECILIA TAN, $10.95
The first book in the series, a little goth "pillow book," with a lot of gender-bending vampires and raw intensity.

Low Budget Gems

TECHNOSEX: CYBER AGE EROTICA, ED. BY CECILIA TAN, $7.95
High technology means better sex toys! Seven hot stories on the cutting edge of technological eroticism, from VR to AI and more.

OF PRINCES AND BEAUTIES: ADULT EROTIC FAERIE TALES, EDITED BY CECILIA TAN, $7.95
Bawdy, phallocentric, sexy tales with gay and straight themes.

FORGED BONDS, ED. BY CECILIA TAN, $4.95
Bondage fantasies set in worlds populated by elves and humans alike, exploring the erotic freedom in slavehood.

TELEPATHS DON'T NEED SAFEWORDS, CECILIA TAN, $2.95
Published in 1992, these three short stories of mostly heterosexual S/M science fiction marked Cecilia Tan's auspicious debut as an erotic writer. "Stirring indeed!"—*Factsheet Five*

VIRTUAL GIRLS: THE EROTIC GEMS OF EVAN HOLLANDER, $6.95 "T&A with G-force!" says Kyle Stone, "A provocative peep show," says Amarantha Knight. These are five of Evan Hollander's best science fiction sex stories.

QUEER DESTINIES, A CHAPBOOK OF EROTIC SCIENCE FICTION BY GARY BOWEN, $5.95
A smorgasbord of homoerotic fantastical stories by the author of *Diary of a Vampire*.

The Ultra Violet Library

Our new imprint of gay & lesbian science fiction. Sensual but NOT explicit:

THE DRAG QUEEN OF ELFLAND, LAWRENCE SCHIMEL, $10.95.
Short stories full of wit and pathos, exploring both queerness and the mysteries of magic: a lesbian bookstore owner learns to run with the werewolves, a drag queen discovers he is the lost heir to faerie. "[Schimel] has a tremendous facility for inventive plot situations and a very pleasing prose style."—The Magazine of Fantasy & Science Fiction

THINGS INVISIBLE TO SEE: GAY AND LESBIAN TALES OF MAGIC REALISM, EDITED BY LAWRENCE SCHIMEL, $12.95
Top contemporary authors (Sarah Schulman, Nancy Springer, Leslea Newman, Rand B. Lee, and more) explore the hidden layers of reality under queer existence. "...Schimel displays the clean prose, fresh eye and ticklish imagination that have brightened his star as both a writer and anthologist."—Publishers Weekly

Ordering Instructions

1. Fill out the list of books you want, with prices, and compute your subtotal.

2. If you are a Massachusetts resident, add 5% sales tax.

3. If you are within the continental US or Canada, add $3.50 shipping and handling for the first book, $1.25 for each additional book. (Books are shipped via First Class mail.) If you are in Europe, add $5.00 for the first book and $2 for each additional book. If you are in Asia, Australia or elsewhere on the Earth, add $7 for the first book and $2 for each additional book. (Overseas books are shipped via Global Priority Airmail.) If you are on another planet, we're very sorry, but the Interplanetary Delivery strike has interrupted service to other quadrants.

4. Add your subtotals together to get a TOTAL, and send in this completed form with the TOTAL amount in US Dollars by check or money order made out to "Circlet Press." Mail to: Circlet Press, 1770 Mass. Ave. #278, Cambridge, MA 02140

If you have questions about your order, please e-mail to circlet-order@circlet.com or call us at (617) 864-0492, office hours noon to 4pm Eastern, Monday through Friday.

Circlet Press on the web: http://www.circlet.com

ORDER FORM

Send books to:
Name: _____

Address: _____

_____

City: _____ State: ___ Zip: _____

Phone: (_____) ____ - _____

Email: _____

Your signature below is required or your order cannot be processed.

"Yes, I am over the age of 18 years old and wish to receive material of an adult nature in the mail."
Signed: X_____

Please Send Me The Following Books:

Title	Price
Subtotal	
MA Resident Tax 5%	
Shipping Costs	
TOTAL	

Send orders to Circlet Press, Dept. FF, 1770 Mass. Ave #278, Cambridge., MA 02140